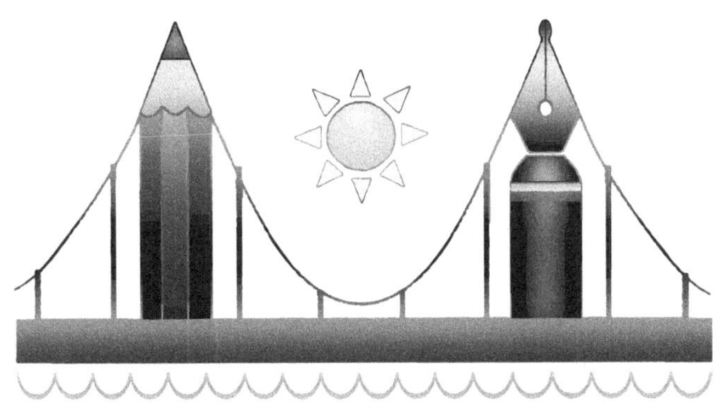

SAN FRANCISCO WRITERS CONFERENCE

2021 WRITING CONTEST ANTHOLOGY

First Edition

Designed and Produced by E. A. Provost at
New Alexandria Creative Group
For the San Francisco Writers Conference
Anthology ©Copyright 2021 by the San Francisco Writers Conference
All rights reserved by the individual authors.
www.NewAlexandriaCG.com
www.SFWriters.org
Available everywhere via print on demand.
Please support your local bookstores.
ISBN: 978-1-64715-003-7

Dear Reader,

Each year for the last 15 years, the San Francisco Writers Conference held a writing contest to help aspiring authors rise above the crowd and catch the attention of agents and publishers. While acknowledgment and prizes were always awarded, those managing the contest lamented that they and the judges were the only ones to actually read the finalist entries. We have wanted for many years to offer you the opportunity to share our delight in discovering the work of these up-and-coming authors. This anthology is the fulfillment of a request/suggestion made so frequently we can't enumerate it.

Entries were limited to the first 1500 words of an unpublished manuscript, or up to 3 poems with a collective word count within that. That's about how much time a writer gets to entice an agent, so this is an opportunity for all aspiring authors to see what a good first impression looks like. We hope that you will be enticed to seek out the rest of their work as they achieve greater things in the coming years.

CONGRATULATIONS! To each of our finalists and especially our grand prize and category winners and runners up. We look forward to reading more from and about you in the future. Every year we have speakers at the conference whose careers really took off after becoming part of our community as contest finalists, scholarship winners, regular attendees, or volunteers. We hope you achieve keynote level renown and come back to share what you've learned on your path to becoming the writer you want to be.

THANK YOU! To every writer who submitted work, we cannot hold a contest without broad participation. You are an essential part of our community and we hope you will continue to improve and submit. Persistence is the number one factor in achieving success as a author. To our volunteers and judges, you made this contest happen. To New Alexandria Creative Group, who partnered with us to publish this anthology, you made a dream come true.

We are grateful that through this season where a pandemic kept us at a distance, canceling our main conference for the first time, your stories still brought us together. The world will always need more. Keep writing.

Sincerely,

The San Francisco Writers Conference Executive Board

Find out more about the San Francisco Writers Conference and our year-round events, including the next writing contest, at SFWriters.org.

Table of Contents

POETRY

This Girl..8

San Francisco, how I hate and need thee, how you
   hurt and heal me 10

Headland Ghosts...12

I Laid My Son To Rest 15

DNA..16

diary of a dead eel boy.......................................17

Lost..19

The Wind is Cruel..20

Short-listed 22

A Scape 23

CHILDREN'S & YOUNG ADULT

Golden Secrets 26

Gorges, Nevada..30

Butterfly Dreams: A Monarch Butterfly's Life Cycle ...34

Kingdom of Lies 35

Refugees in the New World — Gaby's Quest 40

The Ghost of Bentley Manor, A DeeDee Palmer
   Mystery, ...44

The Keystone: Finding Home 48

The Nesting..52

The Wrath of Queens 56

Virtuosity Village 60

ADULT NONFICTION

Fireweed: A Memoir.. 66

The Creole Incident 70

Falling Into Fire 73

How We Fall In Love 77

I Got You Babe 81

Liar, Utah.. 84

Crosswalk Analysis 88

Something to Talk About 92

Under Foot 95

White Dress 97

ADULT FICTION

The Unseen 100

The Burden Keeper 105

Rotten... 109

Falling to the Middle 113

48 States... 117

Last Sunrise... 121

The Beckoning.. 123

The Beginning.. 127

The Interim Solution... 130

Tiger in the Night... 134

POETRY

This Girl

Spring comes, and I am
    unhappy again.

I am always unhappy.

They are always the same.

Those eyes,

the heat behind them,

their shaky hands,

itching for the meat of me again.

I am picking their desire
    out like cherry pits,

rolling them around in the
    palm of my hand,

sticky skin drawn red.

When will I want?

When will I want so much,

so desperately,

my hands shake,

so hard,

I don't know where to place them.

In June, the devil beats his wife.

With bare feet against
    warm concrete,

I wait for you to arrive.

I have spent all day carefully
    curating the way I will
    appear before you,

pressed hot oil into the
    crook of my neck,

so that I will appear
    malleable to the eye,

like the skin of an overripe lemon.

When your lips touch mine,

you will taste brown sugar,

the sweat on my upper lip,

and how bad I want you to want me.

Later that night,

on soft cotton,

I will cry when your hands
    find the place where fat
    squishes up on my hip.

But you will only see the
    way that I bend,

that I fold into you,

pale seaglass held in a child's hand,

only pull me closer when the
    moonlight finds my bare skin,

and it goes right through me.

In July, the bugs come.

I watch one, blood drunk,
    land on his thigh.

I am sitting by the water
    when I meet him,

toes dragging shapes
    through the current.

There is sunlight falling
    onto my bare skin,

and I watch as his eyes won't
    leave the spot where my
    shoulder meets my neck.

I stare back at him,

cold and hard.

That night with lips laced
    red from wine,

when his hand can't stop seeking
    out the stretch of skin that
    shows when my shirt rides up,

like a thing run wild,

I decide I want.

This is where he takes.

Afterwards, I dance around
    him in the sand,

grains of it spraying up
    around my ankles,

and he asks why I can't be
    like the other girls,

with their clean clean skin,

their flushed cheeks,

their soft smiles.

I am picking out dirt
    from underneath my
    fingernails when I say:

I am.

Sonia Del Rivo graduated from Carnegie Mellon University in 2019. Follow @sdrpoetry on Instagram for more.

SAN FRANCISCO, HOW I HATE AND NEED THEE, HOW YOU HURT AND HEAL ME

CATEGORY RUNNER UP

How can it cost this much money to occupy space?

One bedroom in a house
   full of bedrooms
   full of people you don't know $1200/month

One minute late
  to move your car out the way
    of the street sweepers +$100/not every month, but shit, it's hard in a pandemic, being told not to leave but expected to move, confronting, running at 9am, the dude writing a ticket, refusing to dismiss it, we are in nothing together, every man lavish or scraping by, for himself

Unaware of a newly placed
  construction sign?
   My partner paid +$600 for the space a car takes up in an impound, call it $590 if it's your first time, call it *newcomer's discount*

          +$7 if you leave, to return to our seven by seven square, call it 7 times a month, call it 49

It's just crazy because
  I didn't
  choose to be alive
  I mean I choose it every day, ($63/day, for food, shelter, electricity)

yet this is the only city
   where I feel safe
    Even in other parts of this ____________
        fucked up expensive state

doctors misdiagnose, mistreat me,
   double check my ID
   to ensure it's possible
     that a man with a vulva
      can exist,
     then still edit
      my chart
      as if to
     make me disappear

And in states like Missouri,
where the rent is cheap
gender-neutral bathrooms are unrequired, + conspire and call it
                "religious protection,"
but bathrooms are not in the Bible, the Bible is an excuse
                to manifest exclusion

and in states like Florida,
   officials are considering,
    ending transgender infiltration
    with simple genital inspection

      of minors
      shoulds + suspicions

Arise, chastise,
   say I decide
   Look— anywhere but here,
     I'll be financially free,
      but what I need will be + denied to me: mental health,
                hormones, at least a feigned
                right to exist

If I get misdiagnosed again
    because healthcare professionals
     think knowledge + excludes trans

If upon my instruction
    of my anatomy, I am called + no longer a man

I would say,
   it's probably not worth it ____________
     for me to have cheap rent

Cal Calamia (he/they) is a queer trans poet, high school teacher, activist, author, and grad student. His first collection *San Franshitshow* was published in 2021 by Nomadic Press. You can grab Cal's book or learn more about him at calcalamia.com or instagram.com/calcalamia.

HEADLAND GHOSTS

My mother drives her decades-old
    red Toyota pickup truck through
    a tunnel that shines a dull orange

And takes a minute to get through
    (I try to hold my breath the
    whole time, for luck. I cannot).

A bright mist swirls around
    the vehicle

As we pass through clumps
    of white houses

Adorned with moss,

Clotheslines hanging with the
    garments of strangers.

An old chapel with a roof
    as red as clay

Pierces through the fog,

Out of place and time,

A guardian too old to protect
    anyone anymore.

A dark lagoon stands still,

Glassy and severe,

As the road curves and

A blurry grey beach comes into view.

My mother kisses my head

When we finally reach
    summer camp.

A lady with dark hair and
    hiking boots

Leads me to the other campers

And I am welcomed somewhere
    strange and new

For the first time.

I am six years old, I have
    never been happier.

The dark-haired lady leads

Fifteen

Rambunctious, tumbling

Disorganized children

To the beach,

Herding us away from
    the water's edge

Like lambs

As we shrilly ask why we can't touch

The ink blue ocean.

She stumbles with her
    words, and tells us

That this is the edge of the world

And I believe her.

Bird bones scatter the lagoon
    like a morbid art piece

Bleached by the sun that
    seldom shows itself

Through the expanses of fog
    that wrap themselves

Around the hills like a frigid quilt.

My eyes water from the piercing cold

As I watch a great blue heron soar,

A blurry petrichor (I could still see
    the colors of smells back then,
    petrichor being grey and blue)
Through my gaze
Flying into the mist.

My ear presses to the trunk
    of a eucalyptus
As I hear the faint trickle of water
Like a rainstick
Course through the bark
    and into the ground
Feeding climbing trails of poison oak
And blackberry
Growing burgundy, summer is
    already fading towards fall

My new friend, a blonde girl
Who, like me, perpetually has
Sticks and leaves matted in her hair,
Tells me we are both witches,
And that she sees ghosts floating
Through thickets of coyote brush
And cypress.
I cry, I do not want to see ghosts.
I am ten years old.

A deer rests in the fog, unspeaking
These trails mean nothing
    to her as she
Chews sage and coyote
    brush with her
Human-like teeth,

I find a sense of odd
    understanding within both
    of our sets of large eyes
I have doe eyes, my mother
    has told me.

Eroding cliffs the color of coyote fur
Form a narrow path to an outlook
Where paw-prints are
    permanently preserved
In concrete
Outside an off-white lighthouse,
Paint-chipping,
Rusted and tired as the dim light
Inside of it eternally glows.

Power lines are overtaken
    by ivy, no longer
Climbing, but now resting
Amongst the wires
A nest for an osprey.
I creep through a tunnel amidst
The blackberry bushes,
Smelling sawdust and
Shrubbery,
A smell I could never quite
    place for too many years.
The clearing in the brush is
My own nest.

Abandoned Batteries,
    concrete structures

An unnatural molted pelt of
    oranges and neon green
    and chipping spray paint
Being overtaken by red and
    green ice plant, a plant never
    meant to be here at all,
Tendrils clinging to the walls
For dear life
Haunted, almost, as if
They'd ever even been properly
    lived in to begin with.

The March water flows
    unwaveringly from the lagoon
To the sea,
Numbing my legs and
    fingers as I chase
My cold friends
Who reek of seaweed and salt
Just as I now do.
I am fourteen.
Otters dart below
The pond's surface,
Racing through feathery reeds
And brown cattails,
Only emerging to glance
    in my direction

With beady eyes,
Dark as the water itself.

A clay-colored coyote leisurely
Saunters into the road,
A silvery fish hanging out his
Fanged mouth.
He stares into my doe-eyes,
Knowing something that I
Used to remember,
But can no longer place.
He trots off into the forest.

I feel my own ghost pacing
    under the crumbling roofs,
Small and soft and unknowing.
I hope that if I reach out, I'll
Somehow remember--no, regain-
The unknowing and
    youth I left here,
That these walls would stand
    forever, unchanging.
I am now sixteen years old.

I am not crying. The wind is just
    stinging my eyes again.

Dylan Gibson is a writer, artist, and filmmaker who lives in the San Francisco Bay Area. They love discarded things, strange animals, and abandoned buildings that nature has taken back. Their flash fiction, *Murmurations*, is forthcoming in Small, Bright Things: 100-Word Stories in the ELA Classroom, and their art has appeared in two recent Walt Disney Family Museum virtual exhibitions. www.dylanagibson.com.

I Laid My Son To Rest

Each snap of thunder over the cemetery
Brought back sounds of bullets
Cutting off his young life.

But I'll go on because that's what Black mothers have always done.

I laid my son to rest today and the angels smiled.
I saw their faces through my tears.

I laid my son to rest today and the wind rejoiced.
I felt its soothing breeze attend my heart.

I laid my son to rest today and paradise welcomed him in full glory.
I witnessed the rainbow from earth to heaven.

I'll celebrate his birthday tomorrow.
And when I blow out the candles,
My wish will be that no mother
Has to celebrate her son's 16th birthday without him.

But I'll go on because that's what Black mothers have always done.

Lois Merriweather Moore is a retired adjunct professor in the University Of San Francisco School of Education. She is the author of the award winning *Voices of Successful African American Men* and editor of *The Dispersion of Africans and African Culture Throughout the World: Essays on the African Diaspora*. Her latest book in progress is *Walking a Path Guided by Your Own Light: A Little Book of Wisdom Thoughts*. Find her online at linkedin and on twitter @loismmoore.

DNA

It was Monday morning, and I
    was passing the big statue
in the lobby of Johns
    Hopkins Hospital
searching for Room 20, for an
    interview with Mrs. Willis

She had a permanent
    smile on her lips
her hands wrinkled with
    red nail polish
Mrs. Willis looked me in the eyes
How do I pronounce
    your name, dear?
I said, MAH NAZ, the
    same way it's written

Mrs. Willis, with her MS
    degree, said I'd try.
MENAZ, Manos, Maha-noss !
then gently she changed
    her voice and
said, Can I call you Mary?

Marry? Merry? Morry?
    Echoed in my head
I felt like evaporating morning dew,
like a branch of a tree
    under heavy rain,
like a fruit just fallen from a tree

I looked Mrs. Willis in
    the eyes and said,
'But my name is the charm
    of the moon,
the name my parent called me
and the man with black hair,
dark mustache and brown eyes.'

Mrs. Willis was looking at me
with open eyes.
I said: Mrs. Willis, is my name
more difficult than
Deoxyribonucleic acid?

Mahnaz Badihian is a poet, painter, and translator whose work has been published in several languages worldwide. She runs the literary magazine *MahMag.org* to bring the world's poetry together. Her latest poetry collection, *Raven Of Isfahan*, was published in 2019. She is a member of the San Francisco RPB (Revolutionary Poet Brigade). In 2018, Mahnaz had three days of an art exhibition in San Francisco. Currently, she is working on her novel, *Gohar*. Her new collection of poems: *Ask The Wind*, will be published in 2022 by Vagabond publishing.

DIARY OF A DEAD EEL BOY

at the wane of day my father and
  I would strike out small in
  tall rush and long shadow
greasy wellies and waders orange
  and blue through kloo-ik kloo-
  ik and a-wick and a-wick

my father and I would navigate
  fruiting bodies upright catkins
  and egg-shaped leaves
down to bat song air at crag point
  o' dark and the one twisted
  ash and succulent grasses

split the green curtain he did with
  his club-fingered hand and
  bid me break my slipping
gait with the sober refrain care is
  the order while hopping goat-
  like scree and rock chimney

at river's edge we left good altitude
  leaned one the other on
  sharp degrees waterward
and entered the lair of the eel down
  to the killing stone mucked
  with bone gut and gill

dark now darker on the face of
  father's eyes flint knives for
  sacrifice and organ dissection
he ran silence through nocturnal
  notes and brackish molecules
  blood spores in the nose

spillers he'd take and drive the
  stakes like a looney railman
  laying bed and ties into the sea
gather line and hook under foot
  and stab a worm fatway short
  to make show of the ends

out went the line and sinker straight
  points aft of entry and father
  and I bent crooked obtuse
and tautness in the hands that
  were the sign of a true lay or
  untold fears coal lorry black

behind him I stumbled hammering
  spare stakes tossing hooks and
  smelling and hearing blind
and always the glup of water and
  kee-ik of little owls and the
  dank of sulphur salt and nettle

through sand and heron shit we
  skittered palm-reading nylon
  and slack for hunger and urge
shoring up spillers and skirting
  carbon rust of hippo tusk and
  macaque jaw and dung beatle

and then he bade me do that thing
  that was holy of holies and
  life for life and seed for seed
but come the shot recoil and
  treadless boots come the slip fall
  and lumbar shock at sedge bar

and bubbling ho! and breathless
   hee! and gasp and pee and neck
   and ice and skin and smart

and entropy and amber trilobite
   and salt shad and mud fart
   and snot jelly and black hole

and father cursing the weight of
   the boy and sinkers of melted
   led and iron pipe and always

the hook and the mouth and the
   boy's leg for anchor and bloody
   minutes cut into his hands

until the earth gave way at the
   bottom of the world to the mud
   golem and the O-mouthed

oily thing wrapped long at his leg
   and father looking fire-eyed
   and hellbent at eel and eel boy

and stomping spineless and clubbing
   paste-wise the jaw eyes and
   tooth plates in its ugly face

and returning next day with the
   sober refrain care is the order
   and spillers worms and hooks

Dean Gessie is an author and poet who has won or placed in more than 100 international competitions. Dean won the Enizagam Poetry Contest in California, the Ageless Authors Poetry Competition in Texas, the Frank O'Hara Poetry Prize in Massachusetts and the Editors' Prize Poetry Contest from the Spoon River Poetry Review in Illinois. Dean's short story collection, called *Anthropocene,* won an Eyelands Book Award in Greece and the Uncollected Press Prize in Maryland. Find him online at amazon.com/author/deangessie.

Lost

We saw him once before,
standing mannequin stiff,
thin arm and wrist extended,
coffee cup in dirty
pleading palms.

Pin-striped businessmen
hurried by. Mothers shushed
gaping children, slapped
pointing fingers as if swatting
pesky lake flies.

Coins clinked, perhaps
for a greasy burger,
not enough to pull
blackened teeth
in a dentist's chair.

My ten-year-old son yanked
his grandma's crisp dollar
from his denim pocket,
solemnly dropped it in the cup
as if his Sunday offering.

Now here he is
curled up on the concrete
below the grimy window
of a cheap souvenir shop.

I wonder how he can sleep
in the blazing sun,
how he doesn't wake
amid the traffic and horns.

And where is the doleful hound
that sat by his side?
Lost and forgotten
like the man who barely lives.

Lost among the scurry
of strangers.

Constance Hanstedt is the author of the memoir *Don't Leave Yet, How My Mother's Alzheimer's Opened My Heart* (She Writes Press, 2015) and of *Treading Water*, a poetry chapbook that will be published in the fall of 2021 by Finishing Line Press. Her poetry explores the integral aspects of family, memory, loss, and atonement. Constance is a member of the California Writers Club, Tri-Valley Branch, where she leads the poetry critique group. Find her online at constancehanstedt.com.

THE WIND IS CRUEL

The wind is cruel
my worst enemy
cuts through the cracks
of this cardboard house
where I'm half living
and half dying
with my best friends
this bottle and this mouse

you may recall a face like mine
a few times a year on TV
eating turkey at the mission
so grateful
around the holidays

The rest of the year
I blend back into the sidewalk
a figure without a name
a statistic
invisible
voiceless

you may not see me
but I can see you
I can hear you
I can hear the little girl asking her mother
"Why is the man sleeping at the doorway?
Why doesn't he go home?"
"He's homeless, dear. He doesn't have a home."
"But why doesn't he have a home?"

"Because he hurt himself in the head long time ago,
and can't take care of himself anymore."
yes, I hurt my head long time ago
in a place far away
and the rest of me followed

The mother puts down a box
in front of my house, and says
"I hope you like pasta, sir.
It is still hot."
but they were gone before I could say:
"Yes, thank you ma'am
I like pasta
I like them hot
someday I'd like to make some pasta
maybe even burn the pot
spill cheese all over the floor
make a big mess from wall to wall
but at least it is my own mess
On my own floor
on my own wall
in a place of my own
a place I can call home
you see, this cardboard house
is really not a home

Ai Mie has been gathering stories across several continents. She writes fiction, non-fiction, plays and poems with a global perspective. She is also a visual artist. She can be contacted at amfwrite2021@gmail.com.

SHORT-LISTED

Tomorrows keep coming,
thanks to prayer,
plans and wishes.
The revolution of time
and nature continues
rotating patterns of force,
affirming forces of pattern.
The paper in our driveway confirms
what we saw yesterday
really took place, validating
that time turns its pages,
displaying the dates,
as though proof of life
in a ransom demand,
holding hostage our
    hopes for return.
One son dead, another hanging
by a kidney needing a match,
a younger brother gone to cancer.

Who are tomorrow's companions
when survival reaches Stage 4
in a process of elimination,
life promises blown flameless
as candles on yesterday's icing?
Morning print unfolds
to reveal that those whose
passing lives we discover
cannot read with us
about themselves today,
the tomorrow that came too late
for them to celebrate
and share our hope for another.
They add new reasons
to work for the priceless dawn
we pray and sleep to greet tomorrow,
one day closer to forever.

John E. Simonds, a retired Honolulu daily newspaper editor, has lived with his family in Hawai'i for 45 years and previously was a reporter for newspapers from Washington, DC, and other cities. Writing poems since the 1970s, he is the author of *Waves from a Time-Zoned Brain* (AuthorHouse 2009), *Footnotes to the Sun* (iUniverse 2015), and a recent third collection, *In a Roundabout Way* (Dorrance 2021). E-mail him at simondsj001@hawaii.rr.com.

A Scape

A brush stirs
Flexing its long thin neck
Bristles stroke the air in readiness
Indeterminate outlines
Of composition

Inky blue dots dart across the canvas
Marks of punctuation
Boldly announcing
A speedy flotilla of dinghies

Billowing sails rippling red
Respond to invisible breezes
Carving tracks of phosphorescence
Through crested white horses
Flecked with hints of turquoise

Shards of vibrant yellow
Beam happily from above
A dapple gold sea shimmers

Filigree shadows dance
Beneath dense foliage emerald green

Tinged with deep orange
Ripening fruit
Weighing heavy on branches
Smudges of ochre and muddy brown
Denoting rocky outcrops
Peek out from a verdant canopy

A gaggle of gangly seabirds
Blotches black as a crow
Amid neutral spaces white as snow
Duck and dive into azure waters
Mottled with patches of purple
Rebounding skyward
Keen flashes of silver
Between their beaks

Anonymous shades of grey
Attempt to subvert clear blue skies
Driven away hastily
To dump hazy pessimism elsewhere
A blot on another landscape
Out of frame
A different easel

Alex Morritt describes his work as that of a 'cultural observer'. His publications to date include travelogues set in Central and South America; a short story collection; a book of quotations with twinned images, and most recently a pandemic inspired collection — *Poetry in a time of Pestilence*. More information about the author can be found on his Goodreads page: www.goodreads.com/alexmorritt.

Children's

&

Young Adult

❧

Golden Secrets

YA HISTORICAL FICTION

Chapter 1

The *hacienda* stood above the *Refugio* harbor on the site of an old Spanish lookout post. The building bricks and roof tiles were crafted by local natives, who witnessed sunken ships, golden treasures, and many a sailor scattered along the Pacific shores in the 1800s. Alicia Ortega lived in that hacienda; today she wore Mama's faded apron and dusted the family altar, praying to Mother Mary, a ceramic saint.

"Help guard our home while Mama and Papa are gone and forgive me for sneaking into my sister's diary."

"Be careful, *cuidate, mija*," Mother Mary said. Alicia backed away from the statue, not wanting to hear the warnings.

A *Chumash* worker, Nina, swept ashes from the hearth. The Ortega family needed household help in the dusty *adobe*. Alicia and Nina were close. Some days they pretended they were sisters.

Alicia was just fourteen years old. She lived with her real sisters, Dolores, the eldest, and Clara, the middle sister; and with their mother and father in the hacienda on the cliff above the Refugio harbor. Then things changed.

"What did Dolores leave behind?" Alicia and Nina scrambled up the stairs to a sleeping loft, a small dim space above the family *sala*. The loft had a bed, a window, and a few pegs on the wall. Nina stooped to collect laundry in Dolores's abandoned room.

"Find rags. Two moons, no rags." Nina lay flat to reach around the sleeping crates, her black braid speckled with lint. Dressed in a stained apron made from a muslin flour sack, she spoke some Spanish, learned from the Franciscans.

"Look." Nina held up a small envelope with handwriting on the flap. "To my sisters." Alicia snatched the envelope and read the note inside.

Dear Sisters,

I am on the way to the Laredo School for Young Ladies. Imagine that, I am now a young lady. I am excited to travel and enroll with the finest girls from the best *familias* in all the northern territories.

Mama and Papa insisted on coming. I apologize for taking them from you. They were in such a hurry to see me off to school. I cannot imagine why. Clara, you can take over my sleeping loft. Alicia, someday you will understand why older girls need privacy. Nina, take good care of my sisters.

I said my goodbyes to dear Captain Harris—my sailor with the ocean blue eyes. Someday soon I will be Mrs. Harris. Also, I gave my confession to *Padre* Romo to prepare for this journey. Write to me when your spelling improves. I may be too busy to respond, but will remember you in my prayers.

Your sister, Dolores

Alicia tossed the letter aside and continued her search of the loft.

"Why are we looking for more rags?"

"Girl make blood—use rags. No rags—girl make baby," Nina mumbled as she searched under the bed and in the clothes hamper.

"But you said Dolores didn't dirty rags for two months. Two moons, I remember." Alicia thrashed through the bedsheets. "What's that mean?"

"Dolores make captain's baby," Nina said. Alicia's face grew hot with the revelation.

Chapter 2

Alicia slumped to the floor and crossed her legs in front of her. She was shaken by the news of how and why girls bled, and the revelation that her sister Dolores was pregnant. She thought back over the events of the previous days.

After Alicia reported the secrets of her sister's diary to Mama, her parents rushed to enroll Dolores in the Laredo School for Young Ladies. No one talked about the Ortega sisters ever going away to school before the diary incident. Alicia repeated a line from the diary to herself. "I lay below and gaze up at Harris, my sailor with his ocean blue eyes." Now the passionate entries discovered in Dolores's journal made more sense.

Nina tugged on Alicia's curls. "You sick? We work now," she said.

"I can't. Why didn't anyone tell me why Dolores was leaving?" Alicia looked around the loft and recalled the days when she looked up to her sisters, even though she never truly felt she understood them.

"Dolores ready to be mama," Nina said. "No worry."

"But Captain Harris? Why pick him? You remember how we snuck peeks at her other boyfriends when we were little?"

"She always like boys. I remember," Nina grinned and sat on the floor next to Alicia. When the two of them started these remembering times it always took a while to finish.

"You're right. She was always eager to meet the boys. Remember when she was caught trying to hold that boy's hand, the young novitiate, Brother Timothy?"

"He left quick, to another mission." Nina felt like part of the family when she shared such memories.

"After that it was Emilio, the clerk who made deliveries to our house once a month." Alicia looked toward Nina, "Did you live here then?"

"*Cierto*, I remember."

"Then, Captain Harris, at Papa's dock—and right away she told Mama she was sure God intended her to give herself over to him."

"She did. I saw them lying on a canvas in a dinghy," Nina said.

"You did? Why didn't you tell me?"

"She made me promise. Said it was her holy service. Your Papa was mad, so I keep quiet," Nina said. "Your Papa say bad things. 'Jesus, Mary and Joseph,' he said."

"Well, now we know the whole story. Dolores is going to this Laredo school."

"With Captain Harris's baby in her belly." Nina tugged on Alicia's arm. "We work now."

Alicia might not understand everything the grownups did, but she intended to guard the family home while her parents were away with Dolores.

Chapter 3

On the same day that Mama and Papa took Dolores away, Captain Harris and other grubby buccaneers off-loaded black-market goods at Papa's dock, Refugio.

"No taxes here, mates, and the bonus is that the harbor master has three daughters! This place is a gold mine." Harris hummed to himself, straightening his tattered coat and turning to the hacienda on the bluff.

Safe from the Spanish harbor taxes of 1805, the wharf was not truly a secret to anyone. Even some of the Mission padres used the dock to bargain for linens, silks, and ornaments.

"Finish unloading the merchandise while I patrol up the hill and inspect Papa's little treasures." Captain Harris reached the *veranda* steps at the hacienda and announced, "I can help Clara run the dock if you let me." He slid his muddy boot close to wedge the door open. Too close.

Alicia saw him approach and leaned against the other side of the door. She and Harris were only inches apart and she studied his face.

"You should not be here," Alicia cried out. "Dolores is not here. Mama and Papa are gone too." No one entered the house when her parents were away, especially not sailors.

Nina helped defend the house by shaking a dust mop through the door's opening. She shooed Harris from the patio with the *manzanita* branch, pine needles glued with pitch to the end. "You go now."

"Why?" Harris laughed. He knew his business at Papa's black-market port was safe. His ragtag crew were only a step above common pirates, but they could slip past the customs officers stationed at the *Presidio*. The distance of Papa's place from the official custom's collectors made it popular as a tax-free landing for *savvy* traders like Captain Harris.

Alicia leaned with all her might against the door. Harris continued to push against the entry like it was some kind of game. He offered Alicia a sly smile. She looked him over. He could be handsome when he washed and shaved, which was seldom. Today he wore ragged dungarees, a patched jacket and a knit cap tugged down over a sunburned face and straggly hair, looking like all the other ruffians. Except for those piercing blue eyes. Something about them signaled that his family was not from Alta California. His expression, full of greed, held Alicia's attention for a moment.

Anita Perez Ferguson, whose achievements are recognized by the US Hispanic Leadership Institute, writes YA historic fiction. Her recent novel, *Golden Secrets*, highlights diverse characters in colonial California. Find her work at anitaperezferguson.com.

Gorges, Nevada

Category Runner Up

The day that my sister Marina and her boyfriend (a real nice guy, she'd said Jameson was, a family man) were killed by a eighteen-wheeler on the highway to Salt Lake City, I was kissing my best friend in the forever-expanding stretch of desert behind Red Saddle Casino. The sky was turning a near-blinding shade of coral as he and I sat in the bed of his dad's beat-up grey Toyota pickup, the metal heated by the now-sinking afternoon sun everywhere our bodies weren't touching, trapping us in our places.

Strands of his black hair were pressed to his face, held there by sweat as he pulled away from me. He stared blankly at the space between my neck and shoulders toward the skyline of russet cliffs and pale salt flats. This had always been a habit of his, averting his gaze at even the briefest notion of shame. It was the same blank stare he'd given his mother when he'd nicked himself on the cheek with his dad's straight razor when we were six, trying to be grown ups by shaving our milk-moustaches. The scar from that day still showed faintly on his skin as I silently sat in front of him, shifting slightly, waiting for him to speak. His hands clasped one another, fingers weaving and unweaving—pickpocket fingers, as my mother would call them, despite Cal being the most honest man I'd ever met.

"Was that okay?" I finally mumbled, the quiet too overwhelming for me to handle.

"I guess," he said back, still looking over my shoulder.

"You guess?"

"I don't know."

"I'm really sorry."

"It was my idea, Jude."

"We can pretend it didn't happen, if you want."

"I don't wanna pretend."

I don't remember what he said after that, though if I had to guess, it was probably nothing at all. There wasn't a whole lot to say, no real way to address the fact that two boys were kissing in the middle of Gorges, Nevada.

By the time I'd walked myself home, the sun was long-set, hidden behind the rusty-orange mountains, leaving the sky a dark indigo as I opened the door of my family's one-story, crate-shaped house. Sun-bleached teal paint chips curled off the door, revealing the original dirt-grey hue that my father had worked tirelessly to cover up when I was in elementary school, only about a year before his heart gave out. The leaves on the plants near the doorway were tinged brown at their edges, suffering either from the hot sun or my mother's inability to remember to watcr them; even our succulents and cacti were dry or dead, though, to my knowledge, they'd always been that way.

The last thing I can remember about that day was the sound of choking, heart-wrenching sobs that trickled through the front door as I opened it.

* * *

"And you're leaving when?" I ask, lying back on Cal's navy blue comforter, staring up at the popcorn-textured ceiling. When we were little kids, we tried to find monsters and dinosaurs in the odd shadows that dimpled the surface.

"Um, today?"

I sit up, cold shock shooting down my spine. "You weren't going to tell me...*any* of this?"

I had to hear from two boys in front of me in line at 7-11 that he's going. Away from here. And to college. We haven't said more than a few words to each other in months. But even *before* that, before everything, he never told me he was even applying. And I didn't consider it. It isn't that he's not smart enough to go to college. He is, and his parents were always pushing him to do our county's ratty little science fair and study far too hard for tests that even our teachers didn't care about. I just never thought he could pay for it.

"Scholarship," he tells me cheerfully. "They liked my essay, I guess. It was pretty surprising. I'm still in shock."

He doesn't look in shock. And I guess my face says what I'm thinking, because he fidgets. That same averted gaze. Those same pickpocket fingers intertwining and untangling from one another. "I just. I knew you were still in shock…" I swear I've never heard him say *in shock* ever before, and now it's the only thing he seems to be able to say. "...About Marina and all, plus—" He closes his mouth silently and throws his bag over his shoulder. "I've gotta do a few things." Meet up with those guys from the 7-11, I assume, who were talking about seeing him later. People I didn't know he's friends with. People *we* were never friends with. "You should come back around seven. I'm leaving around then, whenever Josiah gets here."

Josiah, apparently, is a dude he met on a forum for people going to NorCal University. A dude picking him up on the way.

He zips closed a duffel bag of ratty old t-shirts, the only ones he owns but which I can somehow imagine him donating to a collegetown Goodwill the minute he gets there. He walks out of his room, leaving me alone with his barren walls, devoid now of posters, and his ratty navy bedspread.

I come back to his house at seven, though I barely have to walk, our houses having been just a street away our entire lives, his always far more cared-for than mine, never engulfed in the dust devil that had fallen over my house after my dad died. There was a car out front ("He drives a Chrysler Imperial!" Cal had told me while packing), pale robin's egg blue with silver hubcaps that appeared to be meeting Nevada dust for the first time in their lives. Outside the car, Josiah Carter is talking to Cal as Cal lifts his single duffle bag into the car, leaning against the passenger-side door and combing his dirty blonde hair nonchalantly with his hand. He notices me before Cal does, waving a polite hello, taking his weight off the car as he stands up straight, brushing the specks of grime off of his khaki pants (a horrible choice for Nevada heat).

"You must be the famous Jude I've heard so much about!" He grins as he says it, though something about his expression makes the compliment feel rehearsed.

Cal finally looks up, startled, shutting the car trunk loudly. "Oh! Jude! I didn't think I'd see you again!"

I don't need to see his hands to know he's lying. I smile half-heartedly, the same way I've been smiling at neighbors for months as they ask gingerly how I've been doing

"since...well...you know."

"I just wanted to see you one last time before you abandon me." I laugh, though it isn't a joke.

"We're just about to leave. You got here in time," he says as he clears his throat, walking over to me with a certain caution, hesitant, like I'm a feral animal. He opens his mouth again, like he has something to say, but he doesn't utter a word. I grab his hand suddenly, squeezing it in my palm. He pulls away the moment I loosen my grip, staring like I've hit him.

"C'mon, we don't have many hours of sunlight left!" Josiah yells from inside the car, though I didn't notice him get in.

"Well. Um." Cal stares at the space between my neck and shoulders, only this time the cliffs and salt flats aren't behind me.

Until now, even with the months of silence between us, I'd been convinced that if I only wanted that boy enough, the world would eventually give him to me. But as the car door slams shut and the sound of Josiah Carter's Chrysler Imperial fades away down the road, I know all at once that my absence will not make him any fonder of me; that in his rush of college parties and old money and new clothes, I'll be forgotten altogether in the depths of his memory, tucked within a blurry nest of glimmering casinos and cigarette butts and strip malls and rows of dust-stained trailers.

Dylan Gibson is a writer, artist, and filmmaker who lives in the San Francisco Bay Area. They love discarded things, strange animals, and abandoned buildings that nature has taken back. Their flash fiction, "Murmurations," is forthcoming in *Small, Bright Things: 100-Word Stories in the ELA Classroom*, and their art has appeared in two recent Walt Disney Family Museum virtual exhibitions. Find out more at dylanagibson.com.

Butterfly Dreams: A Monarch Butterfly's Life Cycle

This 230-word lyrical, STEM, nonfiction picture book is written from a new perspective, engaging young audiences with short lines of rhyme and suspenseful page turns. Though soothing, the book's heart conveys the need to care for our planet.

Why should we care about monarchs? These butterflies are bioindicators, meaning they are sensitive to changes in the world. They give people information about the health of the environment. Monarchs depend on plants throughout their lives and are sensitive to changes in the temperature. A decline in the number of monarchs can be a sign that there are bigger problems in an ecosystem and their numbers have dropped dramatically.

Monarchs are international creatures, migrating up to 3,000 miles, from Canada through the US to Mexico. They do not see borders and neither should we.

This summary is in lieu of the entry as it has been picked up by an agent and it out on submissions. Congratulations to Christine and we look forward to seeing the book when it reaches print.

Christine Van Zandt hasn't found fossilized underwear (yet!), but loves digging up ideas that make great books for kids such as her funny nonfiction picture book *A Brief History of Underpants* (becker&mayer! kids, 2021). She lives in Los Angeles, California, with her family and a monarch butterfly sanctuary. Find her online at christinevanzandt.com.

Kingdom of Lies

Chapter One

The old man had been dead so long his skin resembled hardened wax. Like the wrinkled apricots that grew down in the twelfth quarter, once we remembered how to cultivate them.

"Found 'em this mornin'," the Fetcher who'd brought him in said. Her name was Lorn, or something like that. Skin stained with dirt, teeth as filthy brown as the ends of her hair.

Lorn picked up one of the old man's arms off the steel table and dropped it with a dull thud. "Pulled him outta one of the aqueducts. Stuffed himself in real good. Got his arms and legs tangled into knots before he breathed his last."

An uncharacteristic look of mourning crossed her face. "He didn't think about what would happen when the flow got clogged. Didn't he think we'd go looking?"

"He was dying," I said. "He probably wasn't thinking."

I went over to the sheet neatly folded on the side of the table, unfurled it and draped it over the old man's body, covering everything except his head and neck.

Lorn smirked. "Don't think he's got much dignity now that's he's dead."

"Doesn't hurt much, either," I said.

Her grin dropped. She forced a jerky nod. "As you say."

She hated agreeing with me, an apprentice Reclaimer. And I hated being one, just as much as I had when I'd turned sixteen a year ago. I might have grown up in that year, might be taller than most boys my age, my hair might have changed from the blond of my youth to a bristly jet black, but it was times like this that I still felt every bit a child.

"I hope when your mentor gets here you find something good within 'em," Lorn said. "For your sake."

I glanced sharply at her, but she merely rocked back on her heels, thumbs hooked through the belt of her pants. Compared to my loose-fitting robe all apprentices wore, her clothes looked downright unbearable. I'd worn similar when my class had taken a trip to the agriculture quarter. It'd been like wearing sawdust crawling with termites.

"Well now," Lorn drawled on, "don't matter what he was tryin' to hide from us, does it?"

Her eyes flickered to me when I didn't answer, as though I had a clue why runners stuffed themselves into aqueducts instead of giving their memories to the Collective. I couldn't pull my eyes off the man. Off the dead flesh on cold steel.

I was no stranger to death. Reclaimers could only pull memories from the dead, after all. But it didn't mean I had to like it. I hoped, whoever this man was, he hadn't suffered. I hoped none of them suffered. Every time I was here I imagined myself on that table, waxy and cold, with strangers prodding me.

I shivered.

"Don't feel too bad," Lorn said, misinterpreting my shudder. "They're cowards. The worst kind of selfish."

She reached out to pick up the man's arm again. My hand caught her wrist and squeezed, hard.

"Don't touch him," I said. "You'll contaminate his body more than you already have."

Lorn's other hand drifted toward the side of her belt, to where all Fetchers carried their curved knives. Knives perfect for cutting metal, rope, flesh. Anything they needed to get to their chosen prey.

I squeezed harder, daring her to try it.

Then Lorn grinned. I counted two missing teeth before she yanked her arm from my grasp. I smelled rot on her breath as she stepped closer, dropping her voice low.

"Don't be feelin' sorry for him. Not when he tried keepin' all that knowledge from the rest of us. Those memories, those are for all of us, don't you know that?"

"He knows," said a cold voice behind me, chilling my blood, scraping down every knob of my spine.

My mentor, Nazar Valis, slipped into the room quick as a breath. He acted every bit as regal as his Reclaimer position allowed, and looked every bit as dead as the bodies we worked with. His eyes were shrunken in his skull, his skin pale as a grub. They didn't make a robe size thin enough for his body, so the one he wore made his arms looked like eels darting out of their holes whenever he dealt out punishment. Which was often.

I lowered my head as I stepped to the side. "Reclaimer Nazar, I was about to—"

"About to what?"

I winced at his tone. Nazar didn't need to talk loudly to get his point across. When he spoke, his words somehow managed to cut right through me. "About to Reclaim this man's memories by yourself?"

I bit my tongue. No point in opening my mouth and giving him another reason to hate me.

"And how," Nazar went on, clearly enjoying my discomfort, "did you plan to take them this time, when you've failed so many times before?"

"I won't fail," I blurted out. "I won't."

"Kid's confident." Lorn chuckled. "Can't fault him for that."

Nazar glared at her.

Lorn swallowed hard. "Right."

She hurried out, giving only a brief nod to excuse herself. Nazar had already turned away to pick distastefully at the sheet covering the old man. "Come over here, Simeon."

I stepped toward him.

"Closer."

I stepped to Nazar's side. His skeletal fingers dug into my shoulder.

"Look at him. What do you see?"

Was this a test? Part of a lesson I hadn't been taught yet? Nazar loved asking me things he knew I didn't know the answer to, delighting in watching me squirm.

I quickly scanned the body, thinking hard on what Nazar likely wanted to hear.

"He's…old. And his hands…" I turned them over. "Calloused. Probably came from one of the lower working quarters. Maybe the mines?"

I licked my dry lips, buying time to think. "Which means…his memories from the Before might contain some ideas on combustion. Maybe a more efficient way of mining he hasn't shared. His subconscious—"

"I see a near waste," Nazar cut through my blathering. His fingers played with the sheet, a sneer on his face. "Why do people like this run, apprentice Simeon?"

I thankfully knew that one. "Selfishness, sir. They don't want to share with the rest of us—"

Nazar raised his hand, and my cheek buzzed in anticipation of the incoming sting.

Instead Nazar placed it on the edge of the table. "Guilt. Shame. Qualities that surface when one is not part of the whole. When someone knows they've done wrong and wish to hoard memories that rightfully belong to all."

I flinched as Nazar stepped aside, one hand pulling me to the center of the table. "He was hiding something. You will find out what."

Then he backed away, as though Reclaiming this man's memories was the easiest thing in the world. My mouth had gone dry again.

"But, Mentor Nazar—by myself, I've never—"

"By yourself."

Now I was really panicking. Surely he knew…surely he had to know…

Of course he knows, idiot, I thought. That's why he's doing this.

I forced myself to raise my chin. "I don't think I can Reclaim alone, Mentor Nazar."

A smile curled on Nazar's lips. "Do you know, Simeon, what use Insrenity has with Reclaimers who can't Reclaim? Do you know what happens to them?"

The words felt like a punch in my gut. I turned back to the table, leaning close.

You can do this. No. You have to do this.

I closed my eyes and opened my mind. I was close enough that I could hear the murmurs of the dead man's memories.

They came in waves like those I imagined were in the oceans of the past, crashing into the shores of my mind. But no matter how much I tried to keep a hold I could never remember what they said, only that just hearing them conjured images and smells and even pain from experiences I'd never had.

I'd mentioned them to Nazar once, but the beating I'd received ensured I never said anything about them again.

I felt the sharp pressure of Nazar's hand on my back. "My patience is thinning."

I pitched forward as he shoved me. I forced my eyes to remain shut but I could smell the man now that I was so close: the hint of preservation fluid. The tint of decay.

All too aware of Nazar's eyes digging into my back, I placed my hand, fingers splayed, above the man's cool forehead.

The moment my fingers touched his skin the memories began, an assault on all my senses, a mass of insanity, like a swarm of bees buzzing in my head.

I slowly narrowed my focus, blocking out the mass of thoughts into manageable bits. Reclaiming was like sifting through a box of mementoes in the dark while wearing gloves, with only a vague sense of size and shape and what you were feeling.

Sean Fletcher was born in the broiling, arid state some people lovingly refer to as Texas. He is the Amazon bestselling author of numerous YA fantasy stories, in addition to other forthcoming books whose characters will not give him a moment's peace until they get their turn in the spotlight. When not making things up, he can be found hiking, biking, or traveling, sometimes all at the same time. Visit him on his website at seanfletcherauthor.com.

REFUGEES IN THE NEW WORLD — GABY'S QUEST

Chapter One

The British had been in Grand Pré for days, an eternity it seemed. The thud of boots and the sharp bark of English words could be heard everywhere. Out in the harbor, their ships lurked, like so many vultures waiting to pounce.

In the bustling little Acadian town, life tried to go on as usual. Indeed, the only concern anyone voiced was that the British looked like they were planning to settle in for the winter. The soldiers seemed to take far too avid an interest in the local harvests.

"Papa says there's nothing to worry about, Perrine." Gabrielle Landry struggled to conceal her annoyance with her younger sister's blubbering.

"But look at the size of those ships. And their rifles have bayonets, Gaby." Perrine's lips trembled.

Gaby raised a finger to her lips to silence Perrine. "I know, I know. Everyone's on edge with this new war between England and France. But we're no threat to the British and they know it, so stop worrying so much." She wished she felt as confident as she sounded.

Ever since the British won the Acadian territories from the French forty-four years ago, in 1711, tensions had been high between the colonists and their new government. Gaby's parents tried to stay out of the political turmoil, but trouble seemed determined to make its way into their lives.

A high-pitched shriek drew Gaby's attention to a small grove of apple trees where her youngest brother and sister had been playing. As the eldest girl in the family, she was supposed to be watching them, but once again, Perrine had distracted her.

"Gaby, Gaby," six-year-old Racine sobbed. "Henri took my doll."

Henri tossed his feathery blond hair, laughed, and shook the doll at Racine. Then he wiggled his butt and took off running across the family's large garden, waving the doll above his head.

"*Mon Dieu,* that boy is going to be the death of me," Gaby muttered. She kicked off her wooden clogs, hiked up her ankle-length woolen skirt, and charged after her brother, doing her best to dance around the turnips and cabbages. She didn't dare take time to circle the garden. At four years of age, Henri could already outrun all of his sisters.

"Henri, *reviens ici*," Gaby shouted. "You better get back here now. *Maman* and Papa will be furious if they have to track you down again."

Well, that was partly true. *Maman* would be furious. Papa would just chuckle, tousle the boy's corn-silk fine locks, and comment on how boys would be boys. Just once, she'd like to hear Papa say that girls would be girls. Why did she have so much responsibility thrust on her? Between minding her siblings and helping with household chores, she had little time to herself. Her older brothers never had to spend their days chasing the little ones.

It could be worse. She thought of her cousin, Olivia, who was married with a darling little boy.

Olivia had recently confided to Gaby that she had another babe coming in about six months. "I can't believe it," Olivia had moaned as she bounced her seven-month-old son, David, on her knee. "Between Davy and the housework, I never have time for me. I thought getting married was so romantic, and I do love Georges, but I feel like an old woman already. And I'm only seventeen."

At fourteen, Gaby was of marrying age, although most marriages didn't happen until girls were at least sixteen. She hoped she wouldn't marry for a long time to come. Homemaking and children were every girl's future. Gaby understood that. She'd just like a little taste of freedom first.

Gaby's heart began to race as Henri neared the woodlands that lay just beyond the Landrys' farm. If Henri ran in there, he could get into a lot of trouble fast. He could be attacked by a wild animal, or step on one of the traps set by hunters. There was also the rare, but real, possibility that he could be kidnapped by slavers who combed the woods now and then. They searched for Mi'kmaq or Abenaki children, but were not above stealing a stray white child as well. Gaby screamed her brother's name again and pushed her way through the rows of corn that marked the end of the Landrys' farm.

"Here he is, Gabrielle." A musical voice rang with laughter. A pretty, brown-skinned Mi'kmaq girl Gaby's age, with long black braids and a buckskin skirt, emerged from the trees adjacent to the cornfield. She balanced Henri on her hip with one hand while she held Racine's doll out of his reach with the other. "He almost ran into me. *L'enfant sauvage* will run right off the edge of the earth someday." She gave Henri a playful swat on the head with the doll.

"Thanks, Muriel. He's going to wish he was at the end of the earth if he doesn't stop running off on me." Gaby took Henri from Muriel and kissed the top of his head. Holding him around the waist, she turned him upside down, so that his fingertips just brushed the ground. Henri squealed with delight, oblivious to the fright he'd given his sister. After a moment, she turned him upright and perched him on her hip. She put Racine's doll in her skirt pocket, well out of Henri's reach.

"Fortunately, I was nearby." Muriel bent down and picked up a basket of berries she'd been carrying before Henri came along.

The Acadians and the Mi'kmaq got along very well. Unlike the British who drove the native people from their homes and seized their lands, the Acadians viewed the Mi'kmaq as equals, and the two peoples socialized with each other on a regular basis. In turn, the Mi'kmaq had treated the Acadians as good neighbors and helped them survive those trying years as they built their first homes in the New World, far away from their homeland in France. Marriages among the two peoples were common, and indeed, Gaby's father's grandmother had been a full-blooded Mi'kmaq.

While Muriel was Gaby's best friend, the two girls were as opposite in looks as they could be. Muriel's complexion was dark and warm, her hair thick and coarse. Gaby was pale, with the same fine, corn-silk hair as Henri, and light, periwinkle blue eyes.

"You are the Moon and the Sun," Muriel's father, David Tall Trees, would often say in amusement. "So different, and yet inseparable."

Tired of holding her squirming brother, Gaby set Henri on the ground, but kept a tight grip on his hand. "No more running off, you hear?" Henri crinkled his nose but said nothing. Gaby slapped his free hand away as he tried to reach for the doll in her pocket.

Gaby turned back to Muriel. "Is your family still coming to the party for Gisele and Joseph's wedding this weekend?"

"Oh, yes. We wouldn't miss it." Muriel's eyes sparkled with excitement. "Do you think you're ready to dance the wedding *koju'a* with us this time?"

Gaby grinned. Mi'kmaq dances were a highlight of many community celebrations. "Oh, yes. I've been practicing those steps your mother taught us every chance I get. In fact, I've been helping Amélie with them. She may join us, if she feels strong enough."

"Wonderful. The more dancers, the better." Muriel grew quiet for a moment and looked at her feet, seeming almost shy. "Do you think Antoine will be there?"

Antoine was Gaby's sixteen-year-old brother. A tall, handsome young man, he turned the heads of most of the single girls in Grand Pré. Gaby knew, though, that Muriel was the only one he cared about.

"If he knows you're coming, he'll be there, all right." Gaby didn't tell Muriel that Antoine had been pumping her for information, too. That was their secret. Gaby had no doubt that Muriel would become her sister-in-law as soon as Muriel's father would permit. David Tall Trees, however, insisted that his daughter wait until she was sixteen to marry, so for now, Muriel and Antoine were forced to keep a chaste distance.

Henri gave Gaby's skirt a tug. "I want to go home. I'm hungry."

Well, that was no surprise. Henri was always hungry. Gaby reached into a pocket and pulled out a small biscuit. That should keep him content for a while.

"I'd better head home, Muriel," Gaby said. "*Maman* will be expecting me to help with supper."

Muriel nodded and faded into the woods. Gaby waved until she couldn't see her friend any longer.

As she led Henri back through the garden toward their home, Gaby chided him in a mischievous voice. "You can't go running off like that, Henri. The *loup-garou* might get you." She bared her teeth and snarled like a wolf.

Instead of being frightened, Henri tossed his head and laughed. "*Loup-garou. Loup-garou.*" He chortled, stuck his tongue out, and pulled the corners of his mouth as wide as he could.

Kathleen Ward has taught writing to teens and adults for over twenty-five years. A writer in several genres, she has won awards and recognition for her poetry and short stories. *Refugees in the New World—Gaby's Quest* is her debut novel.

The Ghost of Bentley Manor, A DeeDee Palmer Mystery,

Book 1

Chapter 1

It was the loudest burp I'd ever heard. It might have been the loudest burp anyone had ever heard. I mean, a serious record breaking burp exploding from the back of the classroom. At first, I think everyone was in shock. Even Mr. Jamison, the coolest teacher at Garfield Middle School, looked up from grading papers. He lowered his reading glasses and searched the room like a Navy seal tracking a national security threat. Everyone turned and laughed. That's when I realized they were looking at me.

It'd been six months since we'd moved to Whitefish, Montana, but I was still considered the weird, new girl, with red hair the color of a burning bush in the fall and freckles as thick as a crowd at an Olivia Rodrigo concert. I was also from that place, Lilydale, New York, where all the crazy people live. Everyone asked why my family moved here of all places. I couldn't tell them it was because of me, not if I wanted to keep my secret.

"Ew, gross," Sarah Monroe whispered.

Sarah stared at me from across the room, while twirling shiny, perfect blonde hair between her fingers. She was the most popular girl in the 6th grade, and if I wasn't careful, my life was going to get a whole lot worse, really fast.

Everyone laughed again.

Trying to remain calm and collected, I stared back at Sarah. *She's chewing that piece of gum like Aunt Amy's old goat, Matilda, chews her cud*, I thought, momentarily distracted.

The burst of laughter filled the room again. I looked around, wondering if the best thing to do was to let the whole thing blow over, no pun intended. Then, Ronnie Gentry, the cutest boy this side of the Mississippi, as Grandma Ella would say, glanced in my direction with a complete look of disgust. It was more than I could take. I slid one corner of my mouth to the side and did what any red-blooded American girl would do at a time like this; I nodded toward Deizel Huxley, who was sitting in the desk next to mine. If there was anyone weirder than me, it was Deizel.

Deizel's face turned as white as a ghost. I know, because I've seen ghosts before, lost of them. Then, he pointed a round, pudgy finger in my direction and blurted, "It wasn't me! It was her."

Feeling my heart beating hard and fast in my chest, I tried to work out what to do next. Either Deizel and me were going to do the whole uh huh it was him, huh uh it was her or I was going to have to own up to it and act like I'd just won an award for the loudest burp from a sixth grade girl. I really didn't know which choice would be more humiliating in the end. I mean it was a toss-up.

About the time I'd decided to take the award and was working on a spur of the moment acceptance speech, Mr. Jamison stood up, rounded his desk and headed toward the back of the classroom. As he walked between the rows of desks, the laughing stopped and all eyes were on him. But, his eyes were on me.

I held my breath.

Then, at the very last second his eyes shifted to Deizel.

"Deizel Huxley," Mr. Jamison said. "What do you think you should say after you burp?

"But…" Deizel crossed his arms, scowled, and slumped in the chair. "Excuse me," he said.

Mr. Jamison nodded. "It might be nice if you apologize to Ms. Palmer."

He bolted upright, dropped his jaw and glared at me. His face had turned from ghostly white to, well, redder than my hair. "I'm…," he began. Then, his eyes narrowed. He looked at Mr. Jamison, then back at me.

I kind of wondered if it was the look of pure horror on my face that had stopped him mid-sentence. But, after I thought about it, I was pretty sure it was revenge instead.

Uncrossing his arms, Deizel began again. This time, his tone was different. "I'm sorry, *Ms. Palmer.*"

"There, that wasn't so bad, was it?" Mr. Jamison said as he turned and walked back to his desk.

He returned to grading papers, and I looked at Deizel out of the corner of my eye. Deizel was still glaring at me, contemplating his revenge more than likely. I didn't blame him.

Chapter 2

When the last bell rang, I gathered my up my spiral notebook, math book, and pencil and headed for my locker at the end of the hall. Every few steps I looked over my shoulder, half expecting to see Deizel behind me, all the while bracing for a barrage of humiliation to follow if he was there. But, each time I looked, he was nowhere to be seen in the onslaught of chattering sixth, seventh and eighth graders in a hurry for the spring break.

Finally reaching my locker after having dodged several upper classmen like an NFL wide receiver headed for the goal line, I spun the dial on the combination lock. I hit the three numbers the first time through and flung open the door. None of the teachers had assigned homework during spring break, so all I had to do was stack my books in the locker and grab my backpack. As I pulled it off the hook, I took one last peek around the locker door, searching the swarm of faces coming towards me.

All clear, I thought, closing the door.

I worked my way to the other side of the hall and made my way to the front of the school. Before I knew it, I was out the door, and run-walking down sidewalk toward home. When I made it to 4th Street and Elm, I was out of breath and slowed down. Then, from somewhere from behind me, I heard my name.

Trying to pretend I hadn't heard anything, I kept walking. But, I couldn't ignore the sound of shoes hitting the sidewalk in rapid succession as they grew closer.

"DeeDee! Wait up!"

I stopped and turned just as Willow Cassidy caught up with me.

At four and one-half feet, she was almost two inches taller than me, but we weighed about the same, seventy-five pounds. But, because she was taller, she looked thinner. Her hair was dark brown, her eyes the same. We looked like polar opposites standing side by side.

"Why didn't you stop when I called out to you?" she asked, squatting suddenly to tie her shoe laces.

Out of habit, I checked the laces on my shoes. I was wearing my pink and blue easy on sneakers. I didn't have to worry about tying laces, not like it was a big chore to begin with, but still it was one less thing I had to worry about.

"I didn't know it was you," I said, shrugging my shoulders.

Willow cocked her head to one side, her eyebrows furrowed. "Who else would it be?"

I didn't say anything because she had a point. It wasn't like I had made a lot of friends. I hadn't made any enemies either if I didn't count Sarah, at least not until today. But, Sarah wasn't my fault. Deizel was. We started walking.

Then, it hit her. "Oh," she said. "Deizel, from third period. I heard about that from Dorcus."

Dorcus was Deizel's twin sister.

I rolled my eyes and nodded.

"He doesn't sound anything like me though."

I looked at her. "Maybe, not up close. But, from back there..."

She smiled. "Yeah, you're probably right. And, some of the boys' voices are changing. It's really kind of funny when you think about it--all that squeaking."

We both laughed.

She was quiet for a minute. Then, she tapped my arm with the back of her hand. "It *was* you, *wasn't* it?"

I rolled my head around, eventually nodding.

Then, we both laughed harder.

When we got to Willow's houses, we sat on the front steps.

"Have you got any plans for spring break"? I asked.

"Nah. You?"

"Not really. Mom and Dad are thinking about visiting family back in Lily Dale, maybe even bringing Grandma and Grandpa back with them."

Willow pulled off her backpack and sat it on the porch behind her. "Is that a good thing?"

Across the street from Willow's house was an old abandoned house, with chipped and peeling yellow paint. No one had lived there for over fifty years, at least according to Willow. But, today there was something different about it, and it was suddenly pulling my attention. Then, something caught my eye in the upstairs window. It was the face of a man, and he was looking right at me.

Jane Stewart is a psychic, medium, and co-host of *Ghost 411* podcast. She has self-published a nonfiction book entitled *Clearings,* and her first adult paranormal suspense novel, *Spirit Lake,* was a finalist in the PNWA 2020 Writers Contest. *The Ghost of Bentley Manor* is a MG paranormal mystery with curious, diverse characters that muddle their way clues in an effort to solve one of the town's oldest mysteries.

The Keystone: Finding Home

Chapter 1

Dodging 101

San Francisco, California

I've found one of the best ways to avoid being picked up by the authorities is to just disappear. You sneak out, drop false trails, and double back, and when you are sure no one is following you, you swap out the plates on your vehicle. We always carried backups for Van Ekman, our ancient VW camper. Then, pull out a map, and with no rhyme or reason, pick a new town to call home.

Lather, rinse, repeat.

That's my life—sixteen years as a nomad.

I used to love it, just the three of us, a team, moving to the next adventure. Now, when my dad changes jobs like some people change underwear, it just gives me a stomachache.

Van Ekman lurched and, with a shudder, stalled two feet short of the parking space.

Click. Click. Click. Holding my breath, I reached for the stone on my necklace and closed my eyes as Dad turned the key in the ignition again. *Click.* There was no roar of sound. The engine was dead.

There had been no traffic when we left a pre-dawn Santa Cruz, and we made good time heading south out of the beach city. Soon, we were looping and backtracking to our new destination. Hours later, struggling through congested San Francisco streets, my dad was white-knuckling the steering wheel as he looked for parking. I guess this was our new home. I had little say anymore. I don't know why he picked this city. It's so expensive, and driving was always a mess. Today was the worst. There was probably a big tech conference happening.

We had finally found a parking spot in a private garage. I hoped he didn't plan on staying long because this place was going to cost us a fortune. I mentally counted what I had left of our rent money, about eighty dollars, and I cringed. That wouldn't get us far.

"Okay, that's it." My dad slid out of the driver's seat and left the door open for me to follow. "Grace, let's go. We're late."

"Late?" I asked. He didn't respond. Something on his phone had already caught his attention. He was so easily distracted, and I was starting to wonder if he was depressed again and trying to hide it. We hid so much from each other now.

Turning, I flipped the long mess of my green-streaked hair out of my face and wiggled over the back of my seat and into the back of the van. Using my arms, which were strong from open water swimming, I snaked my tall frame over the neatly labeled and stacked boxes that represented all our earthly possessions. I grabbed the strap of my messenger bag and pulled. It was stuck, so I yanked on the corner of a box until the strap slipped free.

Knowing the passenger door tended to stick, I slid across the front seat and out the driver's door, pausing to push the gear into neutral, dragging the bag behind me.

"What are we late for?" I asked as we both braced against the frame of Van Ekman and pushed. As soon as the van started to roll, I jumped inside and stepped on the pedal, leaning my full weight into it. The brakes squealed in protest but finally relented, and the van stop neatly in the parking spot. Climbing out again, I checked the spacing. We were parked, or rather stalled, between an Audi and a BMW. The roof barely cleared the depressed ceiling of the parking garage. Van Ekman looked like a piece of bark wedged between two gleaming teeth.

Now what? I looked to my dad for direction. His brow was furrowed. His eyes were glued to his phone as he cycled through numbers to send a text, his fingers clumsy on the gadget's miniature keys.

Who was he texting? Neither of us had any friends. We moved around too much, and we were our only family left. He caught me leaning forward to look at the screen and shoved the phone into a frayed pocket in his khakis. We stared at each other.

Weren't we supposed to be in a hurry? The flutters in my stomach felt like guppies swimming around. I took a calming breath and kept my mouth shut as I settled my messenger bag over my shoulder and waited. Finally, Dad broke the silence.

"There are things about your mother's life you don't know…she was different; they all are—" He drew a long shuddering breath. Grief, longing, and fear all crossed his face then, but with a long blink, the emotions disappeared, like a door slamming shut.

Mom? What did she have to do with being in the city today? The churning in my belly grew as it always did when I thought about my mom.

"There's not enough time to explain. I'm so sorry—Grace, I've always meant to tell you, but I didn't know what to say, and now I've waited too long.

Later, I promise, but now, we've got to go." He grabbed my arm and rushed us out of the garage, the pinch of his fingers on my skin an awkward connection I craved as I fumbled along behind him.

Leaving the parking garage, we walked briskly through unfamiliar streets. The chilly, late-morning air held just a hint of salt. *Stars,* I missed the ocean. I paused at the top of a hill, breathing it in. The steep city was laid out around us, an urban quilt in shades of white, the occasional burst of green, and a border of blue that led up to the bridge. My dad trotted back and grabbed my hand, tugging me forward, a not so gentle reminder to keep up. He quickened his pace downhill into tightly packed residential neighborhoods, then up and down again and again, until my legs ached. We finally left the residential streets, the buildings changing to street-facing retail spaces, office buildings, and towering glass skyscrapers. The roads were packed with cars and the sidewalks with pedestrians late to work.

I had an impeccable sense of direction—and was completely lost. It must have been an hour before my dad stopped in front of a coffee shop and spun around. He glanced left, then right, searching for something. Then he looked me right in the eyes.

"Grace, if something happens to me, you need to run. Don't try to help, don't go back to the van, leave everything, and run. Promise me." He was earnest, and his out-of-breath plea ended in a whisper drowned out by the cadence of the city.

"What do you think is going to happen?" I struggled to understand.

"I don't know…something doesn't feel right. It's not like before. When your mom was here, she always seemed to know what was happening. She stayed connected to them. This time…" He trailed off.

When Mom was here, a lot of things were different.

The flow of people on the busy sidewalk cut around us like an ocean current, slamming us together then pulling us apart, testing the elasticity of our frayed connection. The last year held some winners for us in the most-craptastic moments category. I studied the gray in his dark hair and the lines spidering out from the corners of his brown eyes.

He had changed.

I had changed.

And somehow, we just didn't fit together anymore.

Seren Goode writes award-winning young adult science fiction and contemporary stories. She was born with a dream of far-off places and a love of all things alien. Her debut novel, *The Keystone*, redefines what makes a family and explores what it means to be human. Find her online at SerenGoode.com.

THE NESTING

Based on a True Story.

Have you ever seen those Matryoshka dolls where you twist one in half and there is a slightly smaller doll inside? And when you twist that one in half, there is an even smaller doll inside? And when you twist that one in half….you get the picture. In Russian culture, Matryoshka dolls represent family and fertility. But for me, the descending dolls represent a succession of events that led me down a never ending path, turning my soul inside out. The first Matryoshka doll twisted itself open one summer night in 1977. To this day, I have yet to reach the last doll.

Chapter One -

The Initial twist

June 27, 1977

The mercury in the thermometer hovered just above 110°, as the final school bell echoed through the hallways with a sharp pitch that could wake the dead. The year end grades were hand written onto our report cards, and all of the students at Neal Dow were suddenly flooding into the school yard. Summer was my favorite time of year. I was excited about spending the next three months playing in the creek and running through the sprinklers with my best friend Vanessa.

Vanessa was in the same grade as me, but her home room was with Mr. Crandal which was just down the hallway. Vanessa lived with her grandma, Mrs. Harker, in the house to the left of ours. Sometimes she would stay the night at my house, but only if we promised not to stay up until the television stations went off the air. Vanessa was my best friend in the world. We met a couple years ago when her grandmother's dog wandered into our yard and started digging up our dead flower bed. Mrs. Harker made her come over to help me clean up the dirt and replant the dead flowers. We talked about The Bee Gees, The Dukes of Hazzard, and our love for John Denver. We were inseparable ever since that day.

Summers in Chico were notoriously hot and dry with the occasional summer storm that inspired a funnel cloud or two. We had a long summer ahead of us before starting junior high in the fall. The idea of going to a new school with fourteen year olds made me feel so grown up. We would no longer be in the same boring class all day and sitting at the same boring desk. We would be going to different classrooms for every subject and get to store our books in coffin sized lockers in the middle of an endless hallway. The thought of forgetting where my classes were located or going to the wrong class gave me terrible anxiety. I constantly had dreams of losing my schedule and wandering through the hallways trying to find my homeroom. I couldn't wait for the day when I would never have that nightmare again.

Vanessa was waiting for me outside of her classroom door which was on my way to the bike racks. She was so lucky. Her grandmother bought her a brand new ten speed bike for her birthday which had a fancy book rack above the rear wheel that she secured with bungee cords. I never got anything new. My bike was my mom's old three speed which wasn't as nice as Vanessa's bike, but the seat was much bigger and softer. I liked bigger bicycle seats because they were more comfortable. I once asked my dad if he could install a tractor seat on my bike, but he said the saddle rails wouldn't fit. I had no idea what that meant, but I was disappointed that he couldn't make it work.

"Gary Lawler threw up in class right before last bell" said Vanessa.

"Ick. What happened? I asked.

"Dunno. He said he was feeling sick and then he ran to the door, but didn't make it. Mr.

Crandall rang the front office and the janitor came and threw sawdust on it."

"Ugh. That is so gross." I responded.

"The smell. You can't even know. I'm just glad the bell rang and we were out of there."

"I bet. Well, you'll never have to see that classroom or the barfy sawdust again. Say goodbye to our old school."

"Yeah. I'm glad to be out of here, but I can't think too much about it. The thought of going to Jr. High in the fall makes me feel like throwing up, too. I've heard stories."

"What do you mean, stories? What stories?" I asked.

"Tony was talking about it in class. Something called The Smear."

"What's The Smear?" I asked while folding a stick of DoubleMint into my mouth.

"The ninth graders smear the incoming seventh graders. If you're lucky, they just take lipstick and write a number seven on your face," said Vanessa.

"And if you're not lucky?" I asked, although I'm not sure why as I really didn't want to know.

"I've heard they have something called the Bidwell Shampoo where they put your head in the toilet and flush it."

My God. I almost swallowed my gum. Maybe they wouldn't do that to me since I had a short wedge haircut. "They do that to girls?" I asked.

"No no. I think the boys get bad stuff like that. That and they make the boys push a penny down Main Hall with their nose and race each other. The ninth graders make bets over who will win. I think the girls just get lipstick all over their face. And sometimes get butter in their hair."

Before I had even left the school grounds, I was already wishing I had been held back.

As we got to the bike racks, we reached through the accordion steel poles and fished for our combination locks. This was my least favorite part about riding my bike. The process of uncoiling my plastic bike cable was a lot of work, and it somehow always ended up kinking in the wrong direction. The sun was at the highest point in the sky which made our bicycle seats feel like 200 degrees. I was smart enough to wear gauchos that covered most of my legs so the heat wasn't too terrible. Vanessa liked to wear short shorts so the scorching hot seat rubbed against her sweaty legs and was pretty painful.

Without hesitation, Vanessa pulled off one of her tube socks and stretched it over the end of her seat with about 4 inches of material drooping down. It sort of looked like a knitted condom, but Vanessa didn't care. She rode the entire way home with a droopy sock dangling between her legs. I was never so happy to be riding an old three speed with high waisted flares.

Our homes were only about eight blocks from the school yard and all of the streets in between were flat with wide sidewalks. We could pump a few times on the pedals then coast for the rest of the block. The residential streets didn't have any cars riding on them after school so the only traffic we would encounter in the avenues were skateboards and bicycles.

The sidewalks were softly rounded. We rode up and down the curb from the sidewalk to the gutter and back to the sidewalk as a way of making the ride home more interesting. While we were riding, Vanessa wasn't paying attention and she rode over top of the storm drain grating.

Her skinny tires got stuck between the grates and she flipped over the front of the handlebars. She was okay, but she got a really bad raspberry on her shoulder and elbow. After that, she never again rode her bike in the gutter. She also made me promise not to tell Mrs. Harker or she'd have to start wearing a helmet.

Our street ended at a cul-de-sac which we called the keyhole and our houses sat across from the creek that ran through town. During the summer, the creek bed was mostly dry, so we could ride one of the city made bike paths across the creek to shortcut a trip to the bridge. In the spring, the creek filled with water and sometimes flooded if it was a particularly rainy season. A few winters ago, a neighborhood boy named Jay Henshaw drowned in the creek when he tried to cross the water. He underestimated how deep it was and got swept up in the current and was pulled under. I heard they found him a mile down the creek in the fish dam. Whenever we'd walk down to the water in the spring time to skip rocks, my dad would always remind us of Jay as a warning to be careful.

By Keely Reese

THE WRATH OF QUEENS

The diamonds always drew her eye first.

Velia knew she could see a million of them and never get tired of the sight. The jewel of love and strength: nearly unbreakable. Piles of treasure rose halfway to the cavern's low ceiling, packing the space edge to edge with glittering treasures encrusted with a rainbow of gemstones.

Including diamonds.

A steady drip from the ceiling harmonized with their crunching footsteps---or rather *her* crunching footsteps. Though they wore the same sturdy boots, Elysia practically floated along the ground. If she moved closer, Velia bet she'd feel a pocket of air hovering along her friend's feet, dampening the sound.

Cheater.

Motion from across the cavern drew her attention. She relaxed upon noticing Captain Rhea's head bobbing between piles, her gaze scrutinizing each with careful detail. Velia leaned surreptitiously towards her companion. "What makes this amulet so special?" she whispered.

Elysia glanced in Rhea's direction, assuring she was out of earshot. "I don't know, exactly. She claims it's familiar to her---some sort of lost piece she failed to claim a long time ago." A smile teased at her lips, one that once caused Velia's heart to flutter. "Can't say it surprises me that she would force us to rush here over a matter of pride."

"Did she mention what it does?"

"No, but she's rather enthralled with transformation charms lately. Perhaps it's one of those."

Velia covered a giggle with her hand. Their captain certainly enjoyed finding new ways to cause mischief. When she set her sights on a particular treasure, nothing stopped her from obtaining it. Rhea's cabin glittered with thousands of unique trinkets, a thrilling tale accompanying each piece.

Since joining *The Kueila's* crew nearly five years ago, Velia participated in a number of those tales. They traveled the length of The Mortal Sanctuary: every empire, island, and sea gifted life by The Council of Goddesses. Recruited for her shrewd mind and nimble fingers, Rhea relied on Velia to locate the rare and unusual. She collected a variety of rich targets for her crew, thieving from one end of the map to the next.

One of her contacts informed her about the amulet while visiting one of Deravra's southern isles. A man in flashy clothes knocked back glasses of overpriced liquor, babbling about his new-found riches to anyone within earshot. Apparently, he stumbled upon the island by accident when his fishing vessel capsized. He took cover in the first cave he could find, only to find his shelter containing riches beyond his wildest dreams…and then proceeded to not-so-discreetly flaunt his new wealth to his drinking companions.

Ah, the newly rich: they never stayed that way for long

Captain Rhea's curiosity snagged on the amulet in Velia's retelling: a stone *'like fire trapped within a sparkling prison'* suspended from a golden chain. Rhea's face lit up with excitement and determination, and she ordered them to set sail immediately. Luckily, extracting the location only cost a few more glasses of whiskey.

The isle floated a few days out from any port; ships likely passed its shores regularly, unaware of the bounty just off their route. In favor of discretion, only four of them disembarked; passing ships would easily notice a large congregation of pirates wading across the shores. Leaving their first mate— Armel—with the longboat, Velia and Rhea trailed Elysia inland. She led them on a straight path through the trees, following the pull of magic invisible to all but her.

No amount of treasure Velia located measured up to the value of Elysia's skill. As an Etheri, Elysia was both their crew's best kept secret and greatest asset. The only magic-wielding warriors in the world, The Etheri inherited their power from the Goddesses themselves. Their power ranged depending on how thick their bloodlines ran; but even the weakest Etheri were highly coveted by the highest bidder. Rhea managed to hire Elysia before she could be drafted into the Kingdom of Madruel's war with Droque. With *The Kueila* beyond either country's reach, Elysia hid anonymously as a member of their crew.

And frankly, Rhea put her to better use.

Luckily for Velia's nose, Elysia located the cave's mouth only a short distance through the trees. Shadows danced along the jagged edges of tan rock, their torches illuminating the small space in a dim glow. A single, rocky tunnel led through the darkness, only a few inches separating their heads from the rough ceiling. They descended one by one into the small space, the promise of treasure worth the discomfort. Hopefully.

Velia's feet ached in protest by the time the tunnel finally opened into the cavern where they currently stood. "Find the amulet first," Rhea ordered upon arrival. The captain frantically darted down a path to the left. The longer they searched, the stronger an indescribable tension grew in Velia's chest.

With Elysia's reassurance temporarily soothing her concern, Velia distracted herself by filling her satchel with glittering jewels—after her Etheri cleared them of magical danger, naturally. She marveled over several expensive pieces of jewelry, imagining the high price they'd fetch later. "I can't believe he would leave this much here," she mused.

"I hope he grabbed his favorites." Elysia gestured to a particularly small pile to their right, clearly having been foraged. "With the way he handled his liquor, I doubt he assumed that it wouldn't be here upon his return."

"Lucky for us."

Velia's attention constantly shifted from one exotic piece to the next. She didn't notice Elysia stop until her face nearly slammed into her friend's back.

"Captain." Elysia monitored the pile in front of her as Rhea materialized at her side. Elation simmered in Rhea's eyes the moment she spotted her quarry. Following her gaze, Velia studied the golden chain just peeking out from the pile's center. Set in a black, onyx casing, the amulet's square gemstone sparkled in an array of warm colors, cascading together like a personal sunset. The drunk's description hadn't done the amulet justice.

Despite its beauty, concern reignited low in the pit of Velia's stomach.

Elysia's demeanor shifted. The torchlight reflected in her eyes, their usual light-green color darkening a shade; they reminded Velia of jade. "What do you know about this piece?" There was a hardness to Elysia's tone that Velia rarely heard. Her knowledge of magical objects rivaled that of the rest of the crew's combined; that tone meant *back away*.

Rhea attempted to step past; Elysia quickly countered her. Their gazes locked and held, anger sparking within Rhea's eyes. "It's personal," she snapped. "Step aside."

"Personal or not, you need to tell me what you know about it." Elysia's hand twitched at her side. "Otherwise, I can't protect you from it."

"I take disobedience very seriously, Elysia."

"And I will take it extremely personally if this thing kills you."

The captain took a step forward. Despite her unnaturally short stature, authority radiated from her body. Velia shifted on her feet uncomfortably; how Elysia remained unfazed, she had no idea. "My orders are not a request," Rhea hissed. "Lest you forget, you still work for me. I will personally see you off my ship if you do not step aside."

Velia tensed as sparks danced along the tips of Elysia's fingers; they dissipated immediately, but their energy still crackled through the air. Velia almost protested, too, especially as the Etheri rigidly stepped to the side. The emotion swirling in Rhea's eyes paused her objection. Though perhaps a trick of the torchlight, she swore tears lined the captain's eyes as her hand closed around the amulet.

The image of what happened next would be seared in her mind forever.

Rhea's rich, dark skin drained of color while her body convulsed. Blood seeped from every possible place: her eyes, her nostrils, and her lips all swarmed with red. The amulet remained gripped within her grasp, her knuckles turning white from the effort.

Elysia shot forward as if to wrap her arms around the captain's body; she paused inches away, her hands hovering helplessly in front of her.

"What are you doing!?" Velia screamed. "Help her!"

"If I touch her now, you will likely be hauling us both out of here!" Her jade eyes stretched wide, a variety of emotions flashing within them; Velia never saw such fear in her friend's eyes.

Time froze while Rhea convulsed. Velia couldn't clock how long they stood there, helpless. The moment the tremors ceased, Elysia shot forward, catching Rhea beneath her arms before she hit the ground. "Help me!"

Velia hesitated. "But you said---"

"She absorbed the magic; I only feel it in her now."

Velia quickly obeyed, grasping one of the captain's arms. Blood darkened the front of Elysia's tunic, twisting its color into a nasty purple shade. Looping Rhea's arms over each of their shoulders, they managed to haul the captain's weight between them. Elysia led the way into the tunnel, shifting themselves awkwardly to fit in the tight space.

Velia judged they'd climbed half-way back when the ground shook.

Jessie Lovene first developed her love of storytelling through theater. She actively participates in the Bookstagram community, where she has cultivated an incredible book family of 7,000 followers. As a writer with ADHD and a member of the LGBTQ+ community, Jessie is extremely passionate about incorporating mental health and inclusivity into her stories. Jessie can be found at @jessielovenelit on Instagram or at jessielovene.com.

Virtuosity Village

The Cave

The purple ooze seeped off the ceiling of the cave and produced a symphony of pings as it plunked into the glimmering purple pond below. Tukley lay on the bunyuk leaf bed and listened to the never-ending concert of *drip, drip, drip.* Some mornings the drops fell gently and their rhythm became a lullaby that coaxed him back to sleep. But today the pings were very loud, forcing him to bury his head in his pillow to block out the noise. He wished the dripping would stop so he could capture the last few moments of sleep before daylight invaded the cave. But it was no use. Convinced the din wouldn't end soon, Tukley gave up on slumber, tossed the leaves aside and put his feet over the edge of the bed.

Trudging to the pool near the entrance of the cave, he bent over to peer at his reflection. Suddenly his feet slipped. He sprawled out quickly to stop himself to keep from falling into the liquid. As he looked at his now very close reflection, he saw that he was neither comforting nor scary, just ordinary. His black eyes were like glossy marbles bobbing above the button nose. His cheeks weren't rosy but instead a shiny cherry. And his hair! The orange strands grew from the top of his head like a haystack for at least an inch or two and ended in the tiniest hint of a corkscrew curl. He heaved a little sigh of disappointment as he gazed at his boring image, and wondered for buzillionth time why he couldn't be special.

Plop! Something fell from above and splashed into the pool, rippling the surface and ruining any chance he had of examining the rest of his face.

"Kewtzee? Did you do that?"

"Oh sorry, Tukley. I didn't know you were awake. I was just trying to wrap something new with my twine," Kewtzee responded from the alcove that sat just above the pond.

"Be careful!" Tukley chided.

Kewtzee was the only other inhabitant of the cave. He and Tukley had agreed some time ago that it was too good of a cave for just one person. The little alcove above the pond made a perfect place for Kewtzee to spend time all by himself.

It turned out to be a good arrangement. Tukley was often out and about so Kewtzee had plenty of quiet time. He would sit in the alcove day after day, taking his long length of twine, wrapping it around different objects and then unwrapping it again. Over and over again he would do this until he just simply wore the twine to a frazzle. The hours of being wrapped and unwrapped would cause the thread to escape from around the object in protest. The twine would snap apart into nothing but fluff. Tukley never understood how his friend could spend so much time winding twine. He had ceased to ask him about it, assuming it was just Kewtzee's way of dealing with the monsters and ogres in his mind.

Tukley turned his back to the pond, unwilling to wait until the ripple calmed down for another glance at his face. Instead, he looked around the cave trying to find his zappuls on the polished stone floor. Spying them under his bed, he slipped them on his feet and ambled over to the entry way, peering out to see what promises this day might bring.

It was sunny, that was for sure. The light inched into the cave, the golden rays wrapping Tukley in a comforting warmth. The sun must have also warmed the purple ooze that was encapsulated in the ceiling which resulted in the noisy drip. The flowers in the meadow outside also were affected, opening their petals to absorb its beams. Their heady scent escaped and drifted to his nose as he stood in the entrance. He looked longingly at the village that lay down below. It was early enough that no other creatures seemed to be about. The opportunity the day presented made him bubble with excitement.

"Kewtzee! It's really nice and bright out there today. Why don't you come to the village with me?"

"Oh no, Tukley," his cave mate responded warily. "I couldn't possibly go out. What if we saw some of the Flunts?"

"Nobody is outside Kewtzee. This is your chance," Tukley said impatiently, unwilling to deal with Kewtzee's hermit ways yet again. "Come on!"

Kewtzee muttered *Flunts* again, making Tukley pull at his orange strands of hair in frustration. After a couple of tugs, he gently cooed up to the alcove "We can go look for some more twine. You know that your ball is getting pretty frazzled."

Up above something rustled. A small yellow mattress feather floated down, gliding back and forth across the cave. Kewtzee, finally motivated by the thought of some new twine, popped his head over the edge and looked down at Tukley with his sea green eyes.

"Really? Do you think we can find some before the Flunts come out?"

"We can certainly try," said Tukley, exasperated at having to coax Kewtzee out yet again.

A moment later, Kewtzee emerged from the alcove. He stood at the top where some rocky steps stuck out of a mossy wall and descended to the floor.

Next to it in the same stone was hewn a polished semi-circular ramp. Kewtzee stepped over to it and paused a moment. He made his decision, squatted his rounded behind on the top of the ramp, and slid all the way to the floor of the cave, depositing himself at Tukley's feet and nearly bowling him over into the pool. Despite this rapid descent, Kewtzee managed to hang on to the ball of twine tucked underneath his arm.

"Wow, be careful!" Tukley exclaimed, even though he was laughing at avoiding toppling over into the pool a second time this morning.

Kewtzee picked himself up. He was shorter than Tukley by about a foot. Instead of the cherry cheeks, his were a soft pink like the color of primroses in the spring. His hair was like a fluff of blue cotton candy. A few feathers from his bed still clung to his hair, but he seemed quite unaware of these tag-a-longs. Despite his generally pleasing appearance, he made it a point to kick some dirt in the pool, as if hiding from his reflection and leaving himself clueless to the image he presented to the world.

Tukley knew not to mention the feathers to him. He had shared the cave with him long enough to know that a mention of anything that was out of order would just send Kewtzee in a huff back to the alcove for many hours of twine winding and unwinding along with his usual grumbling. The opportunity to drag his friend out of the cave would pass quickly if he didn't move fast. He twirled around to the cave entrance and said, "We better get going if we want to avoid the Flunts."

Kewtzee inhaled deeply, gritted his teeth, gripped his twine and followed Tukley out of the cave.

The Village

Virtuosity Village was nestled just across the meadow from Tukley's cave. The meadow itself was quite enchanting. Patches of flowers adorned the ground like a smattering of tossed bouquets, their scent kissing the air with delightful aromas. Arching bunyuk trees ringed the edges of the field, bowing to the traveling sun and providing oases of shade from the bright rays. The land gently dipped and rolled down to a small brook. There was no water in this low trench although a few flat stepping stones served as a reminder that a stream could reappear. Just on the other side of it, three pebbled roads led into the village. The main thoroughfare was the largest and ran through the center of the town. Two smaller roads serviced the sides, with a multitude of side roads branching out from all of them. Rows of thatched buildings lined the streets. Placed sparsely along them were large boulders almost twenty feet in diameter. They were white in color, almost like alabaster but with veins of black ore running through them. It was their shape that made them unique.

They were rounded on the back side like most large stones, but the side facing front had an indented curvature that created a hollowed-out awning. These structures, called podills, hosted an abundance of events for the entertainment of the villagers.

Some podills were the platforms where thespians standing on them could present delightful little dramas. Others housed dancers who pirouetted and clogged to the delight of onlookers. In some of them, an intricate piece of art could be placed on a stand for admiration and adulation. On occasion, the artist would start with only a blank canvas and skillfully create a painting in front of the onlookers' eyes. But best of all, there were times when crooners and musicians would deliver harmonious songs from the podills.

Diana Reckart is a debut novelist and half-marathoner who likes to create fanciful escapes. Her future endeavors include the sequel *Beyond Virtuosity* and a non-fiction book *Abuelos de Vida*, a recollection of her grandparents' lives beginning in the Mexican revolution and the copper mining towns of Arizona. She is a short story contributor to the *Rozelle Writers Anthology*, "The Matchbook Miles". Learn more about her on Facebook.

ADULT NONFICTION

Fireweed: A Memoir

PROLOGUE

The summer I turned nine, a flash storm trapped my family beneath a skinny lodgepole pine on the Wyoming side of Yellowstone National Park. Rain pelted our bare legs and flooded the Artist Paintpot trail.

My father held Dìdi, my brother, protectively in his arms. Dìdi was nineteen months younger than me. He was known at Duke University as the "Miracle Baby" due to a birth complication he was not supposed to have survived.

"Bà Ba!" I tugged on my father's jacket. His attention was focused on my mother.

Mā Ma stood a few feet away from us, exposed to the elements, beckoning for me to join her. Her hood was down, flapping in the wind like a cape. Her naturally wavy black hair, always kept short, licked the back of her neck like flames. Behind her, wisps of white smoke escaped from a fumarole.

Bà Ba shifted his weight. He was not a fan of Mā Ma's annual national park trips, which she had started when I was four and Dìdi two. While Mā Ma took us hunting for unnamed caves, Bà Ba usually waited in the car and complained: *Why go somewhere with bad Chinese restaurants and get eaten by mosquitoes?*

Lightning ripped across the sky closer and closer as if it was homing in on me. I panicked.

"Xiǎo Qín!" said Mā Ma. She only used my Chinese name—*Little Fragrant Grass*—when she wanted me to pay attention. She pulled her camera from her jacket and studied me through the lens.

I wailed louder.

Then, she broke the tension with laughter. Her smile always made me feel like no matter how messed up life seemed, she knew exactly how to fix it. Once she had tucked her camera away, Mā Ma threw her arms into the storm. She closed her eyes, leaned back, and tried to catch it all on her tongue.

The more the three of us struggled, the more my mother relaxed into the landscape.

"Look," she pointed at the gray sky, undulating like liquid silver. "It's beautiful."

I thought she was beautiful.

CHAPTER 1

On the shore of Trout Lake in Montana's Glacier National Park, rain sorted the ends of my hair into rivulets. The evening's chill skated down my spine and spidered its way to my toes. I planted my feet the way Mā Ma did in Yellowstone but felt the earth give way.

More than one month had passed since Mā Ma's funeral and I still woke each morning to the image of her face, caked with makeup she would've never worn, stripped of the spirit her college friends affectionately nicknamed Xiǎo Là Jiāo (Little Hot Pepper). Mā Ma died at the age of fifty, to the same disease that claimed my eighteen-year-old brother the year before: liver cancer caused by hepatitis B. As soon as we buried Mā Ma, Bà Ba sold our house, purged everything that reminded him of Mā Ma and Dìdi and moved closer to his job. Then he joined a Chinese dating service. My relatives expected me to do the same: Jiā Chǒu Bù Kě Wài Chuán (Don't wash your dirty linens in public). Tell others only about the good things happening in your life. When someone says, "How are you?" Respond, "Fine," especially if things are not because of Miànzi (saving face), a complex social currency embedded in the Asian culture that has to do with worrying about how others perceive you or bringing honor to the family.

As an American Born Chinese, I struggled with Miànzi because it promotes collective interest rather than individual perspective and celebrates lying if it "protects" someone. How could I pretend that I didn't lose my brother *and* mother within three years? How could I say "I'm fine" when Mā Ma died two weeks before I turned twenty-one? Instead of accepting my boyfriend's offer to take me to my first bar, I locked myself in Mā Ma's closet, where beneath the drape of her dresses and coats still marinated in her comforting smell, I mulled over my future. Mā Ma and Dìdi's death had raised the stakes. I felt obligated to accomplish something significant enough to make their deaths worth it, something that might release instead of swallow the grief swelling like a lump in my throat.

After we buried Mā Ma, I applied for a job working at the front desk of Lake McDonald Lodge at Glacier National Park. Among the nearly fifty national parks in the United States and Canada we explored together every summer before Mā Ma and Dìdi died, Glacier was my favorite. Superman had his "Fortress of Solitude" to hide from the world, Glacier was mine.

The Blackfeet call this place the "backbone of the world." The peaks of the Continental Divide separate the major watersheds in North America and drive water to either the Arctic, Pacific, or Atlantic Ocean. It is the only place in America that bears four designations: national park, UNESCO biosphere reserve, international peace park, and World Heritage Site. I had only visited this park once with my family, in 1989 when I was sixteen, but there was something about the mountains and glaciers, a landscape carved by moraines, cirques, and arêtes, that sparked a kinship.

I was born in a North Carolina hospital that no longer exists and raised in cookie-cutter homes throughout Southern California. My ancestors originated in China, but I have never been there. Mā Ma was born in Suzhou, whose winding canals earned the nickname "Venice of the East." She came from a long line of artists. Bà Ba was born in Anhui, where poets and artists flock to admire the twisted pines of Huangshan Mountain. He claims that he is a descendant of Chinese superheroes who glided on water, scaled walls, and skipped across the tips of trees. Bà Ba has visited Anhui several times but when I begged him to take me, he said it was a bad idea, "The communists destroyed everything. You can't even pay respects to your great grandparents." Their graves had been desecrated.

My parents fled Suzhou and Anhui when they were in elementary school, grew up in Taiwan, and came to the United States for college. By the time Mā Ma died, my parents had lived in the United States longer than any other country. I was ten years old when my parents took me to Taiwan. During our visit, I accompanied my cousin, who was a year younger than me, to school one day and accidentally fell asleep at my desk. I woke to the whispers of the entire class crowded around me like I was a frog they had dissected. "Měiguó Rén," they said as if "American" explained my behavior. Minutes later, I watched a Chinese teacher beat a child's hand with a stick. I couldn't wait to return to America.

A product of diaspora, the closest feeling to belonging to a place occurred every summer, as soon as Bà Ba's green Subaru Outback entered the boundaries of a national park. In the front seat, Mā Ma would doze with her camera hanging from her neck. Bà Ba would study her as if she were out of his league. In the back seat, Mā Ma and Bà Ba arranged pillows and blankets into a comfortable bed. When we were small enough to fit in their arms, they carried us slumbering in our pajamas into the car so that by the time we woke to the *thump-a-thump thump* of tires hitting pavement, the adventure we had been dreaming about came true. When we were older, the backseat became our secret spy base, equipped with cameras, a tape recorder, books, maps, and notebooks. We conjured imaginary horses we could ride bareback across sublime landscapes too difficult for us to scale. One moment we were bad-ass heroes, the next undefeated villains.

[Not end of chapter.]

Leslie Hsu Oh is an award-winning writer and photographer whose work has appeared in *Conde Nast Traveler, Fourth Genre, National Geographic, Outside Magazine, Travel + Leisure,* and more. This is an excerpt from her memoir-in-progress. At twenty, Leslie had white water rafted, spelunked, hiked, and ridden on horseback through nearly all the national parks in the US when both her mother and brother die from the same disease. Alienated by her father's cultural beliefs, she turns to the natural world and the indigenous people most intimate to these places for answers. *Fireweed: A Memoir* is a story about making sense of this messy world when you lose everything that made sense. See lesliehsuoh.com or @lesliehsuoh.

THE CREOLE INCIDENT

CATEGORY RUNNER UP

A True American Saga

CHAPTER ONE

Washington, D.C.

In October of 1835, Halley's Comet, as it has every seventy-six years, appeared on an orbit through our solar system. It was widely reported to be visible in the night skies over the eastern seaboard of the United States and was thought by certain individuals then, and is still considered by some today, to be a foreshadowing of certain events. To those who attend to such divination, the comet's appearance can either be a harbinger of good fortune or ill will.

Halley's Comet was first recorded by the Chinese in 240 BCE, and was interpreted as a "broom star," believed to sweep the heavens of evil, while in other parts of the world it was considered to be an omen of calamitous events. It seems the comet's fortune is reliant on which side of an historical moment one observes the phenomena. For example, its appearance in 1066 bode well for William the Conqueror, but not as well for King Harold.

As to whether Halley's Comet foreshadowed events on this particular passage is a matter of interpretation and conjecture. The actual real-world events that did occur, occurred in their usual plodding manner, in that they were relevant and new at the time, but have since become history.

During the celestial visit of 1835 certain events took place that would have an influence on the character and course of history in varying degrees: Hans Christian Anderson published the first four of his 168 tales for children; Charles Darwin, on board the HMS *Beagle*, visited the Galapagos Archipelago; and in London, several short stories by Charles Dickens appeared in a British weekly sporting paper called *Bell's Life in London, and Sporting Chronicle*.

In London, the British Colonial office completed a detailed report concerning the disposition of newly-emancipated slaves in the British West Indies, with particular attention to the resettling of former slaves in the Bahamas, so as to provide "subsistence & receiving the benefit of British Law & Manners…"

Her Majesty's government had recently passed the Slavery Abolition Act of 1833. Prior to the Act, Great Britain had abolished slavery in England in

1787 and instituted the Slave Trade Act in 1807 that outlawed the African slave trade.

The Royal Navy established the West Africa Squadron (or Preventative Squadron) in 1808, the same year the United States made the importation of slaves illegal. Although the Royal Navy was active in suppressing the slave trade, the United States lagged in its enforcement. The boarding by the British of American ships, suspected of participating in the slave trade, was one contributing factor that led to the War of 1812. It would not be until 1862, during the Civil War, that the United States actually tried and hung a slave captain for the crime of illegal slave importation—one Captain Nathaniel Gordon of Portland, Maine.

In 1835, the Royal Navy expanded its enforcement of the Preventative Squadron. It instituted the practice of the seizure of ships that may not have slaves on board but were clearly equipped to store and ship slaves. It was hoped that the newly-expanded enforcement would end the practice of throwing slaves overboard while being pursued by the Preventative Squadron.

It was also in 1835 that the United States ship, *Enterprise*, carrying a cargo of seventy-eight slaves between Alexandria, Virginia and Charleston, South Carolina, was forced by bad weather into the British port of Hamilton, Bermuda. Upon interviewing the slaves, the colonial government freed seventy-two who desired to remain in Bermuda as free people. Suffice it to say; there existed bad feelings between the United States and Her Majesty's government over this and similar incidents.

Other matters of history during the comet's passing further involved the institution of slavery.

In North America, Texas revolted against Mexico. One of the main points of contention regarding the Texas revolt was the fact that the Mexican government did not recognize the institution of slavery. American settlers, who had immigrated into the Texas territory at the invitation of the Mexican government, carried with them their worldly possessions, including their slaves. This affront to Mexican law contributed to the inevitable separation of Texas from Mexico and the establishment of the Republic of Texas.

In New York City, Phineas Taylor Barnum began his career as a showman with the exhibition of Joice Heth, a Black woman and a slave, alleged to be George Washington's childhood nurse and advertised to be over 160 years old.

Another American icon made his appearance during this time period. On November 20th, in Florida, Missouri, Jane Lampton Clemens gave birth to a boy she named Samuel. Ironically, the next time Haley's Comet appeared, Mr. Clemens would pass from the earth after leaving a rich legacy of literature.

Near Fort King (Ocala), Florida, the Second Seminole War began. Major General Thomas Sidney Jesup, the commander in Florida during this period of the Seminole War, declared emphatically: "This is a negro, not an Indian war."

Throughout the Southern slave states of the Union, abolitionists were being expelled and the mailing of anti-slavery propaganda was forbidden, based in large part on a paranoia brought about by the recent Nat Turner slave uprising. John Quincy Adams, then a member of the United States House of Representatives, noted in his diary that in Mississippi "[m]obs are hanging up blacks suspected of insurgency, and whites suspected of abetting them."

In the White House, President Andrew Jackson, who had fought in the first Seminole War, was nearing the end of his second term. Earlier, in January of 1835, an attempt on President Jackson's life took place, the first in American history. But for the moist air that fouled the fine gunpowder in the assailant's pistol, causing the ignition to fail, thus rendering the gun useless, Jackson could have been the first assassinated President. Although frail and not well, Jackson attacked the would-be assassin with his cane and avoided killing the man when the crowd separated Jackson and subdued the perpetrator, Richard Lawrence.

By the time Halley's Comet began to fade into the night sky at the end of December, the Blue Ridge Mountains were blanketed with a mantel of snow as one of the harshest winters in memory firmly established itself throughout the eastern seaboard.

In Congress, a political chill had also set in.

John Hyde Barnard is an author, an historian and a musician. He recently completed his first novel: *The Creole Incident, The beginning of the end of slavery.* It investigates how the Constitution and the Union were saved twenty years prior to the American Civil War, by nineteen individuals—who were all slaves. Find out more at creoleincident.com.

Falling Into Fire

Waiting for a doctor to tell me whether or not I'm going to die shouldn't take this long.

My experience with silence up until this moment has always meant the absence of something, but this silence had a presence. This silence was heavy. It hurt.

The loud buzzing of the light fixtures that plagued me for the last few days is now only drowned out by the booming the wall clock makes as the second hand ticks.

Tick. Boom. Tick. Boom.

I desperately hope that the doctor's hesitance to answer the damn question has less to do with the fact that he doesn't think I want to hear the answer, and more to do with the fact that he's taken aback. Most people don't just come out and ask so directly if they're going to die like that. Most people would have a little more humility. Most people.

My body is exhausted from the daily 3am blood and plasma transfusions, not to mention the camera they stuck up in my ass four days ago, and some hole they drilled in the side of my stomach to drain fluid two days ago.

The fatigue and hallucinations have spent my critical thinking skills. The metal clamps' death-grip hooked into my knuckles connected to this giant beeping machine keep me glued to the cold damp hospital bed. Not that I can go anywhere anyway considering I've been classified as an "escape risk," Which means I've had the privilege of a rotating group of female college interns assigned to sit in my room and watch me, with the sole purpose of alerting the nursing station in case I try to leave. Although the only action I've given these young women is a false alarm when I shot up out of my hospital bed to promptly shit all over myself. It's safe to say that humility left the fucking party quite some time ago.

Tick. Boom. Tick. Boom.

This moment ranks. It definitely ranks.

This moment easily hits number one with a bullet in the category of worst moments in my life.

The irony is not lost on me that just over a year ago, I found my reflective state on the opposite end of the ranking spectrum and awarded a new number one in the greatest moment of my life category: the day of my wedding.

Underneath the summer moon, in a state park situated alongside the Pacific Ocean, the night air was illuminated with a large campfire and Chinese lanterns dangling off the towering redwoods. I watched my new bride, looking a "holy shit" level of stunning, hold the skirt of her dress up to lead her bridesmaids onto the dance floor.

My friend Cody had just kicked off the dance portion of the evening by busting out his trademark "worm" break-dance move. It was the one move he had, and it was a hallmark of his back in high school. He had retired it several years ago, when he came to the stark realization that he was now an overweight man in his mid-30s and slamming his body repeatedly on the ground didn't do him any favors. However, in the spirit of the wedding, and being completely shitfaced, Cody plummeted to the ground in his dress shirt and slacks, face first into the dirt, and executed a somewhat altered version of the worm—probably best described as dragging himself through the dirt in a rhythmic motion.

Cody's reminder that father time catches us all, got a huge roar of approval and applause.

The rest of the wedding party jumped in. Our too-large-for-a-wedding party of twenty plus people consisted of siblings and childhood friends, and a plethora of city officials that included the finance director, two of my former assistants, three current program coordinators, two city department deputies and one future city manager. All drunk off our asses.

The majority of us all had highly prolific roles with the city, which on any other day meant that every move we made was under a microscope. Any behavior exhibited; was usually accompanied by a quick glance over the shoulder to be sure there wasn't any media, council members, or community partners in sight. Perception never stopped any of us from also being completely drunk assholes in the evening though; having behind closed door meetings over drinks was a part of the job. It was the only way any real progress actually got done.

But in this moment, there wasn't an outsider to be found.

Being out in the woods overwhelmed me with an unforeseen sense of freedom and joy that fully consumed me, and to my surprise, compelled me to rip off my dress shirt and jump to the middle of the dance floor. I don't even take my shirt off in the swimming pool. I was four years old the last time my shirt was off in public.

"I got you!" Sam, one of my groomsmen shouted, as he could see the immediate look of regret on my face and tore his shirt off too and started dancing like it was what he was put on earth to do.

The rest of the groomsmen followed our lead, and within seconds were all shirtless and dancing. We were all transformed into drunk kings and queens of the midnight forest.

In short, it was Camelot.

I referenced Camelot quite a bit in those days. I had watched far too many episodes of *Behind the Music* where a band or singer would without fail say something along the lines of "we had Camelot, and we didn't even know it." This of course would be followed by an inevitable reference to hitting rock bottom, usually right before the show cut to commercial, and the narrator would tease that "coming up after the break, the bottom would fall through."

That concept stuck with me, and I sure as hell was going to make sure that we all recognized we had Camelot and should appreciate that it couldn't last forever. I knew I didn't believe my own bullshit though. While I definitely thought we were living in Camelot, I sure as fuck didn't think it was going to end.

It was this backdrop of Camelot that served as the setting for my personal greatest moment.

This moment was as good as it would ever get. After this moment, everything would start to come crashing down in a fiery blaze. A blaze that took Camelot with it.

It wasn't too long after when I would fall from grace. More of a swan dive from grace really.

I would hit a very public rock bottom, which would lead to my decision to quit my position with the city, and ultimately leave my Northern California hometown all together.

I would embark on a personal journey with the mission of finding a sense of peace and identity. My intention was to live out my own version of *Eat. Pray. Love,* although the result more resembled that of *Leaving Las Vegas.*

Truthfully, I probably could have benefited from actually just moving to Vegas to drink myself to death after the first rock bottom. Instead, I took the show on the road and according to Google Maps tracker, over the course of 20,186 miles, I drunkenly fell through one rock bottom after the other. I found rock bottoms in San Francisco, Boston, New York, Oregon, Africa and back again.

I had hit so many rock bottoms that I had gone through the rock, the earth's crust, mantle, molten and outer core. All that was left to fall into was the fire---the burning final stage of hell of the earth's hot inner core.

There were several times in the last year that I wanted to die. I was certain I did. This last rock bottom however actually did it for me.

I finally had my moment of clarity.

I did not want to die. Not now.

Not in a humid sterile hospital room in upstate New York. Not in the middle of an unprecedented global pandemic. Not alone.

Tick. Tick. Tick. Boom. Boom. Boom.

"Am I going to die?" I ask again, in the rare event that he didn't hear me, what with us being the only two people in the room dramatically staring at each other and all.

"Well…" the doctor finally provides a break in the silence, and I feel the rocks from the outer core crumble in my hands, and the flames from the earth's fiery core hit my face. The painful silence may have finally been broken, but after the break, the bottom would fall through.

"Quite frankly," the doctor clears his throat, "we're not sure how you're alive now."

B.S. Millett is a member of the Karuk Tribe, and lives with his family and puppy Lil C, on the Oregon coast. He works in development and planning for a nearby tribe during his daylight hours, and spends his twilight hours on creative writing. He's currently working on a memoir, *Falling into Fire.* You can contact him directly through his website at FallingintoFire.com.

How We Fall In Love

Chapter One
And So, I Walked

Summer 1989

The lid of the vintage sea chest lay heavy on my fingers as I lowered it, my hands escaping just before the wood slammed down. I ran my palm over the bent staves of the arched lid, the rough grain separating with age and dryness. My housemate's coffee table, and my minimalist dresser for the summer.

I perched in the center of her couch—my couch—my low rent bed. The night before, another friend had knelt next to this couch, his warm fingers lifting my breast to his mouth. His touch, like an electric current, had burned a pathway through my gut, cauterizing the gangrenous parts of my soul, lifting pure pink flesh to the surface in a burst of pleasure. Was this not proof that I was safe and beautiful, and the past best forgotten?

He hadn't asked me to come lie with him on the carpet. He did not touch any more than my breast. But I could still see his broad face rising, and the short brown hairs on his pale arms as he reached for me. I could still feel the faint echoes of pleasure in my skin.

He'd left this morning. Home to Amherst, as planned.

My housemate was gone too—off for a week-long training somewhere. Her phone's tight, curling cord twisted away from its wall-mounting. Even if it rang, it wouldn't be for me. Nobody knew my number here.

And now, as night fell, I was alone with my mind.

I tried to focus on the bright reds and greens of her scented candles, cradled in plastic ivy on the living room shelves. I could still see the glint of light on the kitchen counter over my right shoulder, and even the soft drape of curtain on the single window far to my left. It was all still there—*I* was still *here*—present, but fading. Darkness seemed to spiral slowly in from the edges of my mind, memories like the blades of a camera shutter closing out the light.

And so, I walked.

I followed the sidewalk until the cement turned to brick. I turned my back on the high university walls and plunged into the warm pools of light carrying eddies of moviegoers and aimless teens around Harvard Square station.

Nobody knows where I am, I thought. No roommates in town, no campus police, no frat boys, and no—like the summer before—parents waiting up.

I fingered the driver's license in my pocket, nestled against a lone twenty-dollar bill and a couple of quarters—my emergency payphone change. The ID had been a lucky find in the laundry room the day before. Good enough to get me into bars. The photo almost looked like me. A serious looking brunette. *Linda McEwan. May 27, 1963. Just turned 26. Happy Birthday to me.*

Twisted streets came together around wedge-shaped buildings. I slipped through a narrow passage and back out to a wide sweep of sidewalk—almost a plaza—drawn forward by the strum of an acoustic guitar, a harmonica, and something that sounded small and wooden keeping the beat.

I leaned in the semidarkness against a low cement pillar—the kind designed to keep cars from escaping the road.

The guitarist, back-lit by a wide storefront, closed her eyes and leaned back from the mic, her silhouette expanding like a smoke cloud, her voice rising into the night.

I began to dance. First my head, then my shoulders. Finally, I shifted my hip from the pillar and let my whole body follow the beat.

"You like this song."

I looked up and saw a small-faced guy—about my age, I thought—his forehead covered in curls.

"I love dancing," I said.

He looked at me.

I took his hand and—although he stood quite still—I danced.

I held his hand lightly in mine, twirled myself under his arm.

Finally, he laughed, and began to dance with me.

"Dude," a voice said from behind me, "dinner."

My dance partner smiled at me with closed lips. He let his hand linger in mine for just a moment before slowly drawing it away.

"Enchiladas await," he said. "Enjoy your dance."

"I shall," I said. I closed my eyes and continued to move, alone now. "I shall."

I danced, my arms floating free, my chest lifted by the soaring soprano. And, as her voice faded out, giving way to the simple strumming of her fingers, my hips and shoulders still swayed. I danced until, finally, she was silent, and the smoke clouds settled back into my bones.

And then, I walked.

I followed the uneven bricks beneath my feet, the sparkle of headlights in darkened storefronts, the intimacy of the voices (so many voices) rising, fading, blending, and, sometimes, finding their way to me.

"Can you spare a quarter," a blond dread-locked teen asked, "so I can build a nuclear bomb?" I slid my two quarters into his hand, relinquishing my payphone lifeline. I had nothing to lose but myself.

The humid air lifted me like a soft breath, as though I had no weight.

Flashing cacti flanked the red neon words: *Welcome to the Border Café.*

I walked past the "Please wait to be seated" sign, down a long ramp that bisected the dining area and emptied into the bar. I slid Linda McEwan's ID and my twenty-dollar bill onto the bar and let the bartender continue where my roommate's wine had left off. Cold margarita under the Corona sign. Brain freeze. A shot. Salt. Lime.

And then, back up the ramp—just halfway—to where the dining tables hovered above as though on a low stage. The guy with the curly hair—his eyes wider in the light—was squeezed in among friends at a table for eight.

"Fancy meeting you here," I said.

The guy next to him snickered.

I didn't care.

An hour later, I rolled over onto my side in the grass and smiled.

"Holy shit," he said.

I laughed. "Shhh!" I whispered, "don't wake the neighbors."

I'd left the restaurant. He'd found me later, back in the plaza, just as the band was packing up for the night. He stood a few feet away from me. Alone. Watching.

I nodded.

He walked over. He put his palm on my hip.

I let myself float slightly forward.

What is freely given, I thought, *cannot be taken by force.*

I led him down a more secluded street, wading into the liquid shadows that ran rapids among the street lamps and trees. An unlatched gate protected nothing but the faded moonlight on the grass.

A blow job, I decided.

The courtyard gate swung open silently with my touch and I pushed him gently to the ground.

"Are you sure?" he asked.

"Fuck, yes."

Lisa Fabish is co-founder of Yale Women Writers and a freelance writer with published works in *Epoch Literary Review, miniskirt magazine,* and more. She is delightfully smitten with her girlfriend and two cats in Northern California. Twitter: @lisafabishwrite | lisafabish.com.

I Got You Babe

I'd never been so high in my life. Because I'd never been high. In fact, I'm not entirely positive I was high. Was a single edible enough to get someone high? Did people even say "high" anymore?

It was supposed to relax me, calm me down. Henry and Hayley brought three of them over, plus a can of soup since I hadn't eaten anything in 10 hours. When I let them in, they presented the gummy edibles like precious jewels.

I'm not a complete loser, I've been offered drugs *dozens* of times. Okay, maybe not dozens. Maybe just the one dozen, because after that people kinda got the hint that I was always gonna say no. I wasn't even gonna pass the joint, because I wasn't gonna touch it. Someone was going to have to awkwardly stand up to either retrieve or deliver it to whoever was going next.

Not me.

But Henry and Hayley had brought the edibles, which are expensive, right? And my heart was concussing itself against my ribs, and if I was going to get high at any point in my life, this was probably the time to do it. Thankfully I was all cried out by that point. I popped one of the edibles into my mouth and tried to untense my entire body.

Then the waiting game continued.

I had already talked to my husband's brother. I had talked to my husband's father. I had sobbed on the floor of our apartment's hallway, more scared than I'd ever been in my life. Our taxes were sitting unfinished on my laptop. The one piece of information I needed--Brandon's Oregon State ID number--still missing.

Henry had texted me not long before, saying he was on his way over. I hadn't seen him in months. Hayley, too. I felt grateful that the situation had already been relayed to them, that I didn't have to explain it. Instead, I took the edible and stood, jaw clenched, in the spot where the kitchen met the living room. Where linoleum turned abruptly to the same ugly, beige carpet every landlord in Portland seemed to use.

Henry got to work heating up the soup. I think it was vegetable. But I was very busy clutching my phone, waiting for the call to come in. For the screen to light up, for Brandon's picture to appear alongside his name. The picture was a decade old, from when his dirty blonde hair was almost to his shoulders. We were kids back then, practically. I mean, we were adults, legally, but what the fuck did we know about being adults?

This? Right here? This was what being an adult was. Taking a single edible so you don't break down in front of your friends.

There was small talk. There had to be, because I don't remember it being silent. That maybe would have been too much for me, especially since I'd been living in silence for five months. For the fifth time, I checked the volume on the phone. Turned up all the way. There was no way I was going to miss his call.

No way.

I fought against the images my mind conjured up. He was with another woman. He'd decided to fly to New York or Georgia or Illinois to work on a job with his web friends. His brother, his father, Henry, and Hayley were all playing a cruel joke on me, pretending they didn't know where he was. Maybe Brandon had planned it that way. Maybe any second now they'd realize how seriously I was taking this, and they'd pull out the cake they'd baked as a surprise.

A surprise... in the middle of April.

The phone rang, and we all went quiet. I retreated fully into the living room, sinking into our ancient maroon couch.

Brandon's name on the screen.

Brandon's photo on the screen.

The phone buzzing and twinkling in my hands.

I answered. "Brandon?"

"Robin." He said my name like he was a million miles away. A galaxy away. Deep under the ocean, or high up on Mt. Everest. "What's happening?"

He had to have seen them, the missed calls from his dad, his brother. Me. Henry. Mike, probably. I didn't know who else his dad called.

"I needed your ID number. For our taxes," I explained. "I called your brother and told him to wake you up. He said you weren't there."

"No," Brandon said, almost immediately. "I'm not there."

So it was true. The place I thought he'd been for the last four months. His brother's apartment in Los Angeles. He'd told me about walking his brother's dog, accompanying his brother to the ER during a panic attack. Visiting his aunt and uncle, whom he hadn't seen in years. Camping in the desert, under a thousand stars. Visiting his old co-workers at See's Candies.

He wasn't there. He'd *never* been there. None of it was real.

I could hardly breathe. The edible was not doing shit for me. But I was determined to know the truth. I deserved that much, didn't I? And whatever the truth was, high or not, I would take it the fuck on.

With both hands, I held tight to the phone like it was the only thing keeping me tethered to the earth. And into it, I whispered, "Where are you?"

Robin Herrera is the author of *Hope is a Ferris Wheel*, which came out in 2014 from Amulet Books and received a starred review from School Library Journal. She lives just outside of Portland, Oregon, and enjoys hard cider, comics, and duck ponds. She is currently working on a memoir. Learn more about her at robinherrera.com.

Liar, Utah

1

Nevada Is for Losers

"Your mother's on the phone," Sasha said. She wasn't smiling. She never smiled. The crucifix hanging from her neck glistened in the fluorescent light and bounced against her collar bones. They jutted out and I wondered what it would be like to be naturally thin instead of relying on laxatives and cocaine.

I sighed and Sasha gave me a look, one that said, "Are you being disrespectful? Do I need to address this in some punitive way that will bring joy into my life?" I smiled, and then she walked me down the hall to the nurse's station where we took all our phone calls, where they could monitor what we said and if we swore or yelled.

The girls in line glared at me – I was cutting and they'd been waiting. It wasn't like I was doing this on purpose. It wasn't like I *wanted* or even *asked* to talk to my mother. Even after being in a lockdown facility with bad roommates and bad food and too much therapy, I still wasn't *homesick* homesick.

When we got to the phone, Sasha waited for me to pick the receiver up off the counter. She watched until I said, "Hello?" even though I knew who it was, and then I watched as she walked back to the ward.

"Hi, honey," my mother said. She sounded like she was trying too hard to be cheerful. She tried to sound cheerful every time we spoke on the phone, like everything was great with me here in the lockdown facility.

"Hi, Mom. What's up?"

"I have news," she said. She took a breath before she told me that I'd finally be leaving this shitty facility in shitty Reno. From what I saw of the self-proclaimed Biggest Little City in the World, it was no wonder so many girls ended up here. Dusty sadness floated around the city, like some giant orb of shitty shit.

But anyway, my mother said that after three long months, I'd finally be leaving *Elm River*. She said all of this with that same cheery tone, like she was telling me we were going to Disneyland.

But we weren't going to Disneyland. *I* was going to Utah. A group home. With some other shitty name that was meant to inspire. *Alpine Teen Center*. My mother then said it was in a real house and that I'd be able to go outside and see grass and experience fresh air. She expressed more excited tension as she went down the list of things I should be excited about, like the fact that there would be fewer girls – an assumption that they were selective.

This was not supposed to be what happened next, going from one institution to the next. Wandering from local psych ward to Reno lockdown to Utah group home. The deal was supposed to be that I spend six weeks in Reno, long enough to get my record expunged and clean myself up, then I could come home and start over. Leaving Elm River should have been great, it should have been the thing I'd been wanting since I arrived 88 days ago (read: not six weeks ago).

But no. It had been three months. My mother and her boyfriend drove me to Reno on June 19, and 88 days later, I was still here. 88 days in this facility with the most annoying roommates: 14-year-old Kayla who played Sorry! by herself at night while I tried to sleep; 12-year-old Frankie who stole photos of my friends so she could pass them off as her own; 15-year-old Alice who showered so frequently she gave herself lice. I never knew that those little buggies would be attracted to a too-clean scalp, but I definitely learned it after they burned my sheets and washed all of my clothes to get rid of any rogue eggs. I wondered what hell was waiting for me in Utah.

When I hung up with my mother, I asked the staff if I could make another call and when they said yes, I called Stella. The girls in line were getting more and more impatient, but I needed to talk to someone. Stella was one of the few friends I was still allowed to talk to on the phone, another diabetic I met a few years ago at camp. Generally on the up and up, good student, sports, the whole shebang.

When I'd gotten to *Elm River*, I was asked to create a phone list of the people I'd like to call. I pulled out my address book and included all my friends: Maddy, Leanna, Rebecca, Em, Rose, Mike, Paul, etc. When the staff saw my list, they phoned my mother saying something about power dynamics being off. But what did they know? She'd taken me here, hadn't she?

So anyway, I called Stella and told her the news: I wouldn't be coming home anytime soon. That I'd be leaving Reno in two weeks, but only to go to another facility for who knew how long.

She started crying, and then I started crying, and then, through tears, she asked the question that I also would've liked the answer to: "When are you coming home?"

"December, I think," I said. I had no way of knowing. It sounded far enough in the future that surely I could hit this target.

She sighed like she knew I was lying.

I hung up. I didn't know what two weeks later would bring, what this new place would be like. At the very least, I knew what the next two weeks would be like. Going through the halls in silent, single-line formations while the staff unlocked each set of doors: girl's ward, nurse's station, hallway, dining hall/school/therapy room/gym/courtyard/any other physical location within some circle of hell. If we went outside, it was to the "courtyard" – this pit of red dust that was surrounded by a giant brown fence with one single door. Guess what that door was? Locked. Two weeks of goodbye groups and some people pretending to be sad or encouraging or happy. Two weeks of furiously writing letters to let people know I wouldn't be coming home, and to try to remind them I was still alive.

In the 88 days that I'd been in this facility, I'd been given a glimpse into who my real friends were at home. I'd heard sparingly from Em and Rebecca and Rose. A letter here and there. Megan sent me two or three letters, one of which told me she had learned to be a responsible meth-head and that I should have been doing the same. Generally, I tried to be understanding, I really did – I remembered what happened when Nadia got sent away to Utah, it was so easy to forget her. What were they doing without me? In the few letters I got, they told me about parties and tattoos and all the fun they were having.

But the ones I could count on – Stella, Jeremiah, Mike, James, Anna – they were the ones that wrote back, that sent packages. Jeremiah sent printed pages of song lyrics and books of poetry. Stella sent me books, stuffed animals, letters, photos. Of course the staff went through it all. "Rachel, tell your friends they can't send you inappropriate photos," Sasha said. She was holding up a photo of me and Stella wearing shirts short enough to show our belly buttons. We were smiling with our overly glossed lips and straightened blonde hair. Hers was down, and mine was up in a half-pony. Hair wasn't the issue, though. It was the belly buttons. Those overly sexual dips in the middle of our stomachs. Sasha really was the worst. She was tall and slender and severe. If any of the other staff had to go through your stuff, they at least were nice about it. But Sasha? She seemed to enjoy it. At least I'd be rid of her soon enough.

I went back to my room in a good mood, otherwise she might give me negative points – that was how girls got *self-reflection* or some other punishment. So I walked past the tables and chairs in the corner where people rarely sat, past the rows of rooms that held my Nevadan compatriots, then past the rec room that was filled with copies of *Little Women* and The Babysitter's Club and Nancy Drew. Which isn't to say I was above those books, but I was. My good friends and my family sent me packages with entire libraries: *The Joy Luck Club, East of Eden, Of Human Bondage, The Color of Water, Brave New World.* I spent so much time in my room reading that I started to get into trouble. They'd give me negative points for making no effort to socialize, and if

I accrued enough, I'd lose my privileges and wouldn't be able to isolate in my room reading anymore.

Rachel Nielsen is a fiction and creative nonfiction writer from the San Francisco Bay Area. She studied literature and creative writing in Paris before pursuing her MFA in London, where she won the 2019 MFA Creative Writing Prize from Kingston University London. Find her online at rachelnielsenauthor.com.

CROSSWALK ANALYSIS

An observer of human behavior or Sherlock Holmes fan, most likely prides themselves on their insights into personality. It's possible to perceive numerous clues about a person's personality by watching their behavior crossing a street in a crosswalk. Focus on their walking style, posture, speed, body language and facial expressions. These each provide information. Extenuating circumstances do need to be considered. Perhaps the person is injured, blind, a child, pregnant, or extremely old. Barring those circumstances, I stand by these analysis techniques as generally enlightening.

I have waited in cars and watched people pass in front of me and thought, "I like that person. I could be friends with them."

I've also experienced the other extreme where I've thought, "Thank goodness I don't live with that person."

A crosswalk is a fleeting peek into a person's psyche. Do they take as much time as possible to cross, or are they rushed and never looking up? Do they make eye-contact with people in your car as they pass in front? Do they have a jaunty pace, smile, and give a little wave as they walk by?

The smiling-waver would be my choice as a friend. Going slowly is usually a power play, display of dominance or they covet attention. Donning headphones or ear plugs are a hint they don't want personal contact with the outside world. Making eye-contact can be an attempt to display dominance as well, unless they're cute and flirting with you – then it can be somewhat charming. The person with their head down might not be aware of other people at all, has a lot on their minds, is addicted to social media or simply too timid to connect with other human beings. Crossing extremely fast might indicate they are highly competitive or extremely late. Their clothing or what they are carrying, may contribute additional clues about self-esteem or motivation. What would Sherlock perceive?

If I'm walking in a crosswalk and a driver comes up too fast and too close to me, I've always wanted to turn, bang my hands on the hood of their car and yell, "I'm walking here. I'm walking here." a la Dustin Hoffman in *Midnight Cowboy*. I've never done it, but it would be fun, wouldn't it.? (Assuming the car owner has a sense of humor)

We tell ourselves it's not fair to make snap judgments about another person. Perhaps they just heard bad news, or don't feel well. Those might be true. However, we **do** judge by first impressions while telling ourselves we shouldn't. Some psychologists say we use the word "shouldn't" because we're trying to discourage ourselves from our natural inclinations of judging. Making assumptions doesn't seem like the right thing to do, but if we didn't, we might not survive. We train our young to look for cars when crossing the street and to be aware of any potential dangers. They are survival techniques. We all do it, and with some good reason; quick judgments can save our lives.

Experimental studies asked subjects to identify people's personality types by facial information they observed in photographs. They found it only takes a tenth of a second to make a judgment. Even though the subject's conclusions are often prone to error, people persist in making these generalizations about others. It happens in all cultures. The researchers concluded that the consistency of ratings, across cultures and age groups, suggest that humans possess an innate method for creating their first impressions and that it is a mechanism that had evolved within our species.

This theory is strengthened by the evidence that children and babies judge people's faces even before they are socialized. A reassuring find is that infants show empathy towards crying people from a very young age. It's not taught, it's innate.

When my youngest grandchild was five months old, I hadn't seen her for a couple of months. My son, her father, asked if I would go to her room and get her up from nap-time. I walked in quietly, smiled and said, "Hi sweetie." Her little face said it all. She looked at me, her eyes got big with a look of surprise, followed by her little mouth forming a downward pucker, punctuated with a loud howl. I picked her up and she quieted but kept looking, quizzically at me.

I told my son; "She's going to be a genius! Babies usually don't recognize strangers until they're nine months old." She knew I wasn't the person who put her to bed. Babies know strangers. They realize when something is different.

Again, we know we "shouldn't" judge books by their covers, or people by first impressions, but we do. It turns out we're pretty good at it, but not perfect. It has social implications. People with the "right" kind of face are thought to be more capable, likeable, and more intelligent. These opinions can affect careers, social lives, and even legal matters. Humans find people with round baby-like faces appealing. This may have evolved as instincts to protect the young and the very old, who often regress when aging, to baby-like features.

Look at the characters who mesmerize children in television programs and movies. They are round faced with large eyes. Although those facial types are usually thought of as likeable, they may not be considered intelligent or capable. When looking for mating partners, consciously or not, faces that are symmetrical with proper proportions and a healthy appearance are considered desirable for producing strong off-spring.

The fact that humans keep making snap judgments is evidence of its usefulness. If it hadn't been useful, it would have been weeded out during evolution. It serves a purpose in human survival. When the accuracy of these snap judgments is compared with results of objective tests, such as professional personality evaluations, researchers find a better than chance outcome – but not a perfect. There is a risk when people ***always*** consider their snap judgments as accurate.

When we consider the evolutionary aspects of quick appraisals, they make sense. Long ago when humans lived in tribes they could immediately tell if a stranger wandered into their territory. Once people became mobile and started exploring the globe, populations mingled, and it became more difficult to ascertain which people might be trusted and those who might be dangerous. My father was seventeen before he ventured to the next town over from his in the Ozarks. I'm sure he was aware if a stranger came to his town. Times have changed radically. People can be on the other side of the world within hours.

I was in London in 2005 when three bombs were detonated in London's underground trains and a fourth bomb exploded on a near-by double-decker bus. Fifty-two people of 18 different nationalities, all UK residents were killed; more than 700 were injured in the attacks. All four of these explosions were in the area where my theater class was staying. It felt like being in a war zone; helicopters continuously flew overhead, sirens blared as law enforcement officers zoomed in and around streets and sidewalks on motorcycles. Not many people had cell phones then, so we couldn't reach our friends to check on them or tell them we were safe.

One member of our group called her son in the states who told her to avoid being near anyone that looked suspicious or carried backpacks. When we got on the Tube the next day, we looked at each other and laughed. **Everyone** looked suspicious and everybody carried backpacks. London is an extremely diverse city, with every type, shape, and race of people. To avoid diversity in today's world, you would need to stay home.

Although we do have a natural inclination to make rapid judgments in the modern world, we find ourselves with, what the researchers call a *moral injunction*, meaning we try **not** to follow our natural inclinations. Should we stop making snap judgments?

No, they help us survive. We don't get to know or talk to every person we come across; we do need to be alert. What we can do is not act on these quick assumptions and keep an open mind. We can get to know people and keep these judgments from turning into stereotypes, where we believe *that every single* person in a group is alike.

I'm telling you all of this to assure you, I have "evolved" to submit my CROSSWALK ANALYSIS. I stand by my unsubstantiated data. Don't get me started on my DRIVING BEHAVIOR ANALYSIS; where I state that people who don't use their blinkers are sociopaths.

Jody Brady is a student of human behavior. Owning two businesses and traveling have convinced her humans are basically the same worldwide and a sense of humor travels well and is easy to pack. Now she has five grandchildren she can take around the world in books—it costs less. Website: jodywrites.com.

Something to Talk About

I tried not to panic as I realized I had to swim for my life. I put so much time and hard work into this endeavor, I'll be damned if I was gonna die. My heart beat raced, my body tightened, and my hands trembled. I quickly scanned the water, looking for any other swimmer who would hear me if I screamed. Off in the distance, I saw the brightly colored swim caps of other swimmers with their faces submerged in the water. There was no way they would hear me over the sounds of the San Francisco Bay. I was on my own. I submerged my face into the salty, frigid water. While the waves slapped my face, I swam as fast as I could to avoid getting swept by the fast moving current and dragged underneath one of the huge boats near Aquatic Park. With each stroke, I prayed I was putting more and more distance between myself and the boats. When I finally felt the grainy sand of the shore underneath my feet, my pulse slowed, my hands stopped shaking, and I no longer felt like I was going to jump out of my skin. I made it. It wasn't my day to die. Sitting on the beach, I let out a huge sigh and wondered, "What was I thinking when I signed up for this? Do I have what it takes?"

Becoming an Ironman is no small feat. It is the granddaddy of all triathlons with distances of 2.4 miles swimming, 112 miles cycling and 26.2 miles running. It is widely considered the most difficult and challenging one day endurance sport event in the world. It is a test of physical and mental strength. Competitors are on the course for up to seventeen hours with nothing but their thoughts. The sport draws professional world champions but also amateurs who seek to challenge themselves. People from all walks of life, who, for various reasons, decide to pursue the journey of an Ironman.

Approaching my fortieth birthday, I decided I wanted to ring it in in a big way. A birthday party? Nah, I can do that anytime and I'm not a party kinda gal anyway. Skydiving? Been there, done that. Hmm, what can I do that would be momentous yet original? I enjoy the outdoors and physical activity. Then it occurred to me. I didn't know how to swim and I hated to run. I'll do an Ironman. It doesn't get any bigger or crazier. Happy birthday to me.

Truth be told, deep down, there was another reason for chasing the impossible. I wanted to show I made something of my life. That in my forty years, I accomplished something. It wasn't enough that I graduated from U.C. Berkeley with a Masters Degree and have a rewarding career as a social worker. Or that I traveled the world, am financially independent and own my home in none other than overpriced Silicon Valley. Yet, despite all of my success, there was something I hadn't achieved…marriage or children. I hadn't felt inadequate until societal norms cornered me and made it known that I was defective.

My mom was having a conversation with her neighbor who asked, "Is your daughter married?"

"No," my mom replied.

"How strange" the lady said.

Then there was the time my friend Phil tried to play matchmaker. "Hey Nicole, I tried to set you up with my friend Art. I told him about you and how you're successful, funny, pretty, and have a good head on your shoulders. He asked if you've been married and I told him no. Then he asked if you have kids and I said no. He asked what's wrong with you."

I was in a relationship with my high school sweetheart for fourteen years. Throughout our relationship, whenever I would ask if we were ever going to get married, he would respond by telling me that he needed to focus on taking care of his single mother and financially providing for her. In year fourteen, I experienced a My Cousin Vinny movie moment, only it wasn't due to showing up to court in a leather jacket. I realized when he said he did not want to get married because his mom was his priority, he meant it. I could almost hear Vinny saying, "You were serious about that?" Living together until we grew old was what he wanted without the marriage part. I wanted someone to call my husband so I walked away in broken pieces.

Then there was the rebound guy. You know, the person you date after the end of a relationship because the interest they show in you and the attention they give helps boost your confidence and put you back together. One day, Mr. Rebound said to me, "How about we go look for rings today?" I hoped he was referring to buying the Lord of the Rings DVDs but figured that was a stretch. I replied, "How do you know if someone is the one?" That was my way of letting him down without saying, "I don't want to marry you." He never brought it up again but I knew I had to end that relationship because it was not fair to him.

Next was the fiancé who decided to let me in on the fact he was a cocaine addict by waking me up out of a sound sleep shouting my name from the living room, panicked and requesting I take him to the Emergency Room because he had snorted cocaine and his heart was palpitating. In his panic, he asked me to swear that if he lost consciousness, that I would call 911. If that weren't enough, when we arrived at the Emergency Room, he informed me that he was embarrassed to enter the hospital because it was not the first time he had been there for cocaine use.

Could I have been married? Sure. I chose not to be married because I was not in love with Mr. Rebound and had I accepted his proposal, I'd be in an unhappy marriage. If I married Mr. Cocaine, I would have aged ten years in a matter of seconds because being married to a drug addict is not a life I choose for myself. Even so, I grieved the loss of that relationship. There were numerous times I went to my parents' house and through my tears, shared how sad I felt, or called a friend to express my overwhelming sorrow. I soon realized that it was not the loss of the relationship I was grieving, it was loss of the opportunity to be married.

I did not want to have children unless I was married because I have no desire to be a single parent. I've seen what being a single parent entails and that is one of the most difficult jobs ever. I would very much like to be married but if not being willing to settle means there's something wrong with me, then so be it.

I had refused to be defined by whether or not I'd been married or if I had children. Yet, while others were boasting about their children or spouse, I too wanted something to boast about at 40 years old. I felt I had something to prove.

Through my 20's, my friends and family members were having children and or, getting married, in no particular order. I attended countless weddings which included ten stints as a bridesmaid. There was a wedding or two in which I performed my duties as a bridesmaid and as soon as I retreated to my car, I burst into tears at living out "always the bridesmaid but never the bride". Then came the baby showers. Then all the talk about what was happening in the lives of their kids which meant their lives. I wanted to stand gazing into the eyes of my beloved, knowing there was someone in this world that loved me so much he wanted to spend the rest of his life with me. What an amazing feeling that must be. I want my heart to flutter, my stomach to be filled with butterflies, and to feel that nothing else matters in that moment.

Apparently I needed to be more specific to whomever answered that wish because I got what I wanted, just not in the form of a wedding, but instead in an attempt to complete an Ironman.

Nicole Bueno is a psychotherapist in San Jose, California. Her work in progress, *Something to Talk About,* is an inspiring, laugh out loud memoir that captures the quest of a woman who set out to compete in an Ironman triathlon and found herself up against overwhelming odds that lead to an unintended journey of self-transformation. Find her online at nicolebueno.com.

UNDER FOOT

My femurs remember holding the tension of my 10-hour workday just below my hips. My thighs were the barrier between the pain of the floor and the place where my brain might absorb it. My body held dozens of silent conversations with the floor, without my permission. After the store went out of business, I stood in the empty spaces, and feel that floor. It was the source of my memory, the part that kept me sure it had all been real.

That concrete floor was a kind of home to me. The first time we had concrete poured at the Buffalo Ranch, the people in town knew. My parents bought the Buffalo Ranch and the three of us went to live on the land that was named long before we got there, to walk in the tracks of the beasts before us. Fifteen buffalo stayed on with us for a year while their owners worked to rehome them. Mom and I fed them hay through the fence with our bare hands. Their grunts reminded me of warm comforting exchanges with my grandmother, their breath sweet with hay, and black eyes watching me through their fluffy fur.

The first pouring of concrete was our sidewalk. Until the sidewalk, mom had creatively repurposed tree rounds to create a path from our driveway to the front door of our single wide mobile home. They lay in our yard like misplaced slices of bread. They gave our home a quaint, rustic vibe, but they were not a permanent solution. The sidewalk was permanent. It was one of the first steps we took in establishing our home, that could not be reclaimed by the wilderness surrounding us.

A wooden swing and a rope swing lived in our barn above a pile of hay. Some bales were stacked, not yet ripped open to feed the livestock they were intended for. The hay pile meant endless joy for me, climbing the winter woodpile, the thick heavy rope swing in my hand. In a single move, my feet jumped around the knot and I held my breath, gravity sucking me forward.

I was suspended, swinging until I chose the moment to let go and allow my small body to fling into that hay and roll into the dirt. The wood of the rafters where the rope was tied cracked,echoing off the sheet metal.

When Dad poured a foundation in the barn, and my playhouse became his business, Edwing Boats Inc. had already been growing. Dad's wardrobe consisted of flannels and jeans that collected burns and holes from the sparks of the welding guns. Diesel and sweat were part of his permanent chemical makeup a scent he carried with him everywhere. Now the lines were drawn. If I fell on the concrete after a swing, no amount of hay could save me. The swings were cut down, the hay moved out, and I signed my name in the new cement.

When I am three, Mom decides I need to learn to read. She says I have too much energy and there are not enough places for it to go. She tells my father to start reading aloud to me. I remember crawling into his lap and looking at a large bright yellow engine manual as my bedtime story. I didn't understand and it didn't matter. He reads it to me anyway.

One night I bring him a book *I* want to read. It's "Aladdin" and it contains fifteen chapters. Dad tells me he will not read it to me, that I will have to read it to him. "No!" I protest, but we practice every night until I do.

"When you're in college, you'll have to read at least 100 pages a night," he said.

He teaches me how to ride a bike. Every night he runs behind me, a rake jammed into the bars behind my bike seat. He never lets me fall. It is weeks before I realize he is jogging behind me, no longer holding the rake. He teaches me how to drive. He gets out of the truck and places cans in the middle of the road until I can back over them perfectly. We roll down the windows so we can hear the aluminum crunch.

I brought home good report cards that got me into a state university. It was the first Thanksgiving break home from college when my father sat in the dark living room with me and cried. He told me he never finished his first semester at Pacific Lutheran University, dyslexia crippling him. I struggled to understand why staying enrolled for just 10 weeks had been so easy for me, so difficult for my father, and how it meant everything to him that I had done a thing that he could not. Tears wet his soft face until his beard absorbed them.

I couldn't think of what to say to contain him, put him back into a form I could understand. He was my father, the man who never let me quit, by giving me space to fail until I succeeded. He was there with me, letting me know it was okay and to keep going. I know now, he needed to be vulnerable. He was proud of me. He was allowed to cry; to let go of the rake. I wish I'd put my hand on his. I wish I had told him my ladder was his ladder. Until that moment, I didn't understand that I had something Dad didn't. I had the foundation.

Elaina Erola studied English at Western Washington University and is an alumni of Humboldt State University. She holds a Juris Doctorate from Northwestern California University and serves on the Board of Directors for the Mendocino Coast Writer's Conference.

WHITE DRESS

I used to see her out walking, long limbed, golden haired, seventeen years elegant. She was three-years older than I, at a time when such things mattered, when I had no way of knowing if I'd grow from a duckling to a swan like Anne Garret. She had a younger sister. I used to see them in their velvet yard throwing the ball to their border collie. Her house was massive, symmetrical, polished; wrought iron over the cathedral windows, a balcony over the front door, boxwood cut to a flat top on both sides. Her family had ties, or they wouldn't have lived in Memphis's Morningside Park, that much was certain. Families inherited into the historic enclave. Each of the twenty-six houses had a common knowledge story.

Anne Garret went to the all-girls, private school, St. Mary's. I knew little of her beyond that. A high school senior leading a full life didn't have to know the fourteen-year-old across the street. There was nothing in it for her. She was one week shy of graduation and had the white dress to prove it. From my front yard, I spied Anne carrying that plastic covered dress from her car and knew it to be for a ceremony. St. Mary's sent their graduates out into the world in a white dress custom made by a seamstress. I coveted that full-length white dress. It seemed emblematic of a given bright future.

Fourteen was endless. I was inchoate and impatient. I walked the middle of the road, in my state of becoming, neither here nor there. I envied Anne Garret going places. She'd be stepping into the wider world without me, and she had the white dress to prove it. From my perspective, she had the world on a string and a grand life before her.

When news of Anne Garret ricocheted from house to house in Morningside Park, it was the first time I'd ever been blindsided. In my sheltered world, I knew little of life's usurping tragedies, and even less of chance and impermanence. My neighbors spoke in hushed voices in a series of intractable images: a rainy night, a swerve to a ditch, Anne's best friend driving. Her friend survived the car accident, but Anne died instantly. In the face of the tragedy, talk throughout the neighborhood concerned how Anne's family should receive Anne's best friend—should they embrace or shun her?

A darkness palled Anne Garret's house when I walked past it. There was an eerie stillness, a dormant front yard, an unspeakable weight on the street. I never crossed the street with my condolences. I didn't attend the funeral, but I was deeply affected by Anne Garret's death. The color changed in my fourteen-year-old world, and with it my false sense of security.

What astounded me was Anne's mother's choice for her daughter to wear in her casket. From my front yard, I spied Anne's parents taking Anne's dress to the car, and it spoke to me of prescient things tinged with notes of the uncanny. Anne would lie in the fullness of youth, golden, and seventeen years elegant. She'd lie on the brink of graduation forever, and she had the white dress to prove it.

Claire Fullerton is the traditionally published author of four, multiple award-winning novels and one novella. She has recently completed her fifth manuscript. Her work has appeared in numerous magazines including *Celtic Life International* and *The Dead Mule School of Southern Literature*. She hails from Memphis, Tennessee, and now lives in Malibu, California. Find out about Claire's work at clairefullerton.com

ADULT

FICTION

THE UNSEEN

GRAND PRIZE WINNER

Sonia

White

Despite their best attempts, I'm not dead.

Blue

I dip my head underwater.

The grit of riverbank sand digs into my kneecaps, and when I burst back out, my long hair arcs a trail of water over me. This is the third morning I've washed in the Mississippi and the fifth day I've been away from home.

Two strangers on a leisure walk avert their eyes when they see me, cloudy water sliding down my skin in thin streams. So far, no one has asked if I'm okay. I've stopped in six stores to buy basic foods and gone to the same library at least ten times to pee. Nobody looks at me.

Grey

Every social worker who came to our house was prettier than the one before. They kept getting younger, too. Every time I told one of them how desperate I was, they promised they'd try to help me. It's a funny thought, needing to promise to try.

There were never lights on in my house. I remember the second to last social worker, her bleach-fried hair sitting loosely in a high bun, kneeling in front of me in the dim living room. I was just a chubby kid, black hair knotted in braids I did myself. They only ever came when my Dad still lived with us, a response triggered by neighbors calling the cops when my mom screamed. The image of that social worker sits in my mind like the shadow of a gargoyle, a fierce watchkeeper, crouched and ready. She's a silhouette. She accomplished nothing.

Ochre

I slap myself in the face to warm up. The temperatures drop low this time of year, and though I've found a soft bed of pine needles between trees to shield the wind, autumn air bites at my cheeks, the only skin on my body exposed. I packed my backpack fast, and haven't changed my clothes since, only added layers on top. Rain jacket over denim jacket over hoodie. Two pairs of socks under my hiking boots.

My palms, covered in flimsy gloves, are flat, not cupped for optimal pain. Just enough to bring blood to the surface. It's pain that doesn't register anymore. Most pain doesn't. The bruises on my shoulders are fading, now speckled in green. The last night at home, Jack held me down so hard, he left tender tattoos of his handprints. Smacks land in a rhythm and I hit harder every few slaps, until my body reacts. I know this warmth. Right now, I'm grateful for any warmth.

Thoughts of what I should do next move to the forefront of my mind, but basic body functions pop them like bubble wrap. It's been a week. One week, and I'm still alive. Cold, but alive. This must be what all animals share, a survival instinct.

Yellow

Nothing prepares you for this. If you come from a life of comfort, it doesn't matter how much, there's no way to imagine sleeping on the streets. Finding a corner somewhere outside and deciding "good enough."

The first night, forcing myself to do it felt like sawing off my own arm. Every single possibility of doom pulsed through me. It didn't make sense. The sun went down and there was still nowhere to go. The first night away from home was pure shock. If I close my eyes, what will come? Nasty urban wildlife? Some serial killer looking for pretty young flesh? The level of exhaustion was so significant, I was paranoid of anything, realistic or not. Possessed clowns. Rabid dogs. All I could do was cry.

But the second night, I laid down on the riverbank and promised myself I'd sleep. Among scattered leaves the color of melted butter, I put everything I could into sleeping. Because it became clear, after only one night, that it was all a mind game. On night two, I repeated a mantra. You're alive. You're safe. You're alive. You're safe.

I wasn't safe.

But it helped to repeat it.

Being a girl alone at night is scary enough, even when you're walking home with 911 on speed dial. When suddenly there was no refuge to head towards, I had to settle into fear.

On Night Nine, more than one week out here, I'm just about asleep when she finds me. The harsh beam from a swinging cell phone flashlight is so bright I can't see who's behind it. I call out, and the beam shifts to the left, showing a side-lit girl with Pollyanna braids. My eyes ache as they adjust to the opposite of the pure darkness I fell asleep in.

"What's your name?" she asks.

"What's yours?" I ask back. Sleep grog blocks my voice.

"I asked you first." And she's next to me, shining her light forward onto the river. Soon the water will solidify. Where will I be by then?

"I'm Sonia," I tell her. Nothing to lose.

"Molly." At the confident announcement of her name, I turn to study her, crouched next to me. Tangled blonde hair twisted into braids. A stomach swollen out to fill the space between her knees.

"You're pregnant." It's been so long since I spoke out loud. It's a struggle just to string together more than two words.

She turns the flashlight off. For the first time since she arrived, I'm uneasy. The lamps on the Stone Arch Bridge, only about a mile away, string along like a beaded necklace through the night. "You're like me, aren't you?"

"Pregnant?"

"A runaway."

"Oh. Yes."

"Of course. Why else would you be sleeping on the riverbank?"

I shrug, but it's too dim for her to see. If I wasn't sleeping outside, if she saw me in the Walgreens, I wonder if she'd be able to tell. I look dirtier than usual, hair streaked with grease, clothes stained with mud. "Can you turn the light back on?"

"Don't want to draw attention."

"They don't look down here."

"Of course they do."

I shift on the damp and clumped up leaves. "Do you have any food?" My jeans stick to my skin, fabric soaked through. My money is running low, and I went to bed with a stomach collapsed into a pit of hunger. Rational-me would be embarrassed to ask, too proud to beg a pregnant stranger to feed me.

"There's some at home."

"You have a house?"

Molly lumbers to her feet, and her protruding tummy nearly tips her over, almost sends her tumbling down the slanted bank. I tilt my head to study her, illuminated by the near-full moon behind her head. Her face is made up, lips red like hard candy and eyes a muddy ring. But she's pretty, in spite of her self-destructive makeup. She's got soft features, and young skin, like mine. "A home." Her hand extends toward me.

"How old are you?"

"You ask a lot of questions."

I slide my hand into hers, her fingernails dirty. She pulls me to my feet and my vision dissolves to black in a headrush. My balance drifts and maybe I'll pass out. Maybe I'll faint into her pregnant belly, bring us both down.

"I'm seventeen." She tells me. "The others call me Mom."

"Others?"

She taps the flashlight on, but covers the phone with her palm, turning the shine orange.

Her light bobs up the hill away from me. "Come on, Sonia."

What are my other options? Nothing, nothing, only slow, broken steps behind her, slippery ground constantly reminding me of the potential to fall. It wouldn't be the worst thing, falling. This is all I can do, accept the seeming kindness of a stranger, because I don't think I can spend any more nights alone. Nothing is safe, but especially not curling up in corners with no one to look out for me. Maybe this Molly, the teenager they call Mom, will look out for me.

And we walk, following the curves of the river like pioneers without maps. We stroll on the river parkway, passing a few runners bundled in form-fitting layers as the darkness is scrubbed from the sky. We cross bridges that are not meant for pedestrians, our bodies hugging the walls, trapping us on the shoulder of the road. All along, I follow a few paces behind Molly. Ready to slip off without a word when I feel like it. For a girl so pregnant she could pop, she moves quick and steady.

We walk through the city for hours, but we don't talk. She speaks to direct me, only once or twice. I don't ask a single question. It's almost light by the time she holds a straight arm in front of me. I run into it, entranced by our rhythm. "C'mon, babe. This is where we go down." Her finger points off the paved path into the brush. I step back to let her lead the way, and then we're climbing down a stamped pathway, over branches and rocks like an obstacle course.

Elena Lee Anderson is an author of upmarket contemporary novels, and founder of the Writing to Wholeness Collective. She facilitates writing workshops with incarcerated women and survivors of gender-based violence. Find her online at elenaleeanderson.wordpress.com.

THE BURDEN KEEPER

CATEGORY WINNER

Juke Joint Johnnie

He was well aware that they were watching him. Staring, in fact, like they did almost every morning. He had never asked them why they lined up their chairs each morning as he arrived at his shop. To ask would mean conversation, and conversation was something he was not allowed.

In his entry process, he appeared to sell all manner of things in his little shop. At least that's the way it was now. It had not always been this way. He had owned and operated many businesses in his life. His shops were always eclectic and contained inventory that changed with the times and perpetually customer based. He could acquire any good, food, or textile instantly upon request, but most of the time, well before one knew it was needed. That was the secret of his thriving popularity. When popularity was required. That's how he knew so much about the chairs. He had sold each one of them in his shop at one time or another. In one place or another. He knew the chairs, but the people in them escaped his recognition, mainly because they did not matter.

He knew they found him suspicious. It was not anything he needed to be afraid of. They could look all they wanted. He knew they could not touch or disrupt him. Still, they sat there. Poised to question, but unable to follow through. Arriving in shifts, each group replacing another. There was no pattern or common number of them. Sometimes there was just one; sometimes there were hundreds or more. He was not allowed to observe the changing of the people in the chairs. They would just appear at irregular intervals as he opened and closed his shop. Looking, but never approaching, never calling out to him, always in the same spot.

It didn't change much. Just the faces and body types and the colors and the clothing and the furniture. At first, they sat on stools from the bar that had been across the street. Then came the bubble chairs and the wingbacks and the clubs and so many he lost count and stopped trying to figure it all out. Even though he had learned so much about them and considered that he was taking on too many of their subtle attributes, he had more important work to do for the universe than to be distracted by any of that. There would certainly have to be a way back from being too much like them, otherwise why was he here? Why had he been here?

The chair group assembled at this point was sitting on that hard cushion French provincial with the carved arm rests. Matching hard ass chairs in that ugly, shiny, loud pink color that everyone of the day they were from was rediscovering in used furniture stores back there and pretending they liked it. He remembered selling a lot of those horrible chairs to people who thought they made them look rich. They just looked uncomfortable to him, even as they tried out the chairs and proclaimed them wonderful and took them home.

Uncomfortable and stupid, that's how they still looked to him, all lined up like that in those atrociously garish chairs.

He preferred the clean lines of handmade wooden furniture; a cushion or two placed in the seating sweet spot was all the chair pampering his mind and body needed. But these people, if that's what they were, always seemed to be sitting on some unnecessary fluff, stuffing or flowered covering that made him think they had to be connected somehow. In his mind they had that one excess in common and he sometimes wondered what else they may be connected to. But mostly they just annoyed the hell out him to the point that some days, he just wanted to walk over and slap each one of them. One by one. Hard, across their ugly mouths. He had the feeling that they would just sit there on those god-awful thrones of theirs and let him do it too. Oh, he was often tempted, but just when he thought he could no longer reach down far enough to find the will to ignore them, he would begin to laugh. Out loud. High and shrill. Laughing freed him somehow; allowed him to continue his assignment. He searched for the connection to his being to the high screech that came from his somewhere, to his ability to move on from the annoying chair people, but a connection just did not seem to be reachable. Whatever brought the laughter had been with him since the start. What he did know, or sense, or feel, was that neither casual nor purposeful interaction was possible or desirable unless arranged.

His interactions were by appointment only.

There was no entry without one.

Even so, the chair people remained. And they kept coming, not trying to enter, just gawking, pointing, and whispering to each other in twisted animation. It was as if they knew they were observing mere seconds of centuries of something. It was as if they thought a clue would emerge, a misstep, a revelation that would help them figure out how to get in. To solve the mystery of the shop. But no such things ever happened or ever would. Not for their eyes anyway.

Most likely, like their ancestors, and their issue, they would not discover much.

They would never know who he was.

That is, unless they found themselves in need the services of a man like him.

A man.

Like him.

That entry made him laugh again.

****

Today was especially sunny. He still marveled at the thing they called the sun. He didn't know all that much about it, but he did know that they had no idea. It was all just warmth and light to them. As he put his key in the door to open the shop, he knew he was drifting from his purpose. But sometimes he had to. It was, after all, a built-in feature to keep him from damage. At least not so much damage that he could no longer function.

It was on sunny, light filled days like this, that he ignored the chair people and entered his store without so much as a glance in their direction. It was on these days that he was able to or directed to refresh and remember why he was here in the first place and the circumstances under which he had first arrived.

The memories did not flood back all at once. Even for him, that would have been devastating. Instead, they came in pieces, fragments seeming to fit the moment and the circumstance. As he opened the door and entered the shop, he felt her presence right away. This would be the first time she had returned since he had arrived. Knowing she would prefer to stand in the shadows, he did not open the blinds on the windows facing the street, leaving the shop darkened.

He walked slowly to the counter and quietly placed his keys on the glass surface. She remained quietly a few feet behind the counter, near the back wall. He didn't quite understand why she was there, but somehow he knew she would not be the first to speak. That was his assignment. For this was not a mere memory. This was a calling. After all this time, she had come back. If had been something he could do he would have sensed her pending arrival. He would have attempted to realign himself sooner and given himself more time to be prepared. But they did not do things according to time. They lived in the life of events and occurrences. He was slowly beginning to come back to that.

He managed to shake off the confines of time and the need for preparation as she sat there in the dark observing him, looking at him unconcerned. Just waiting for him to be ready. She had seen far worse.

He still had a few wantings to shed. He wanted to be released. He wanted to be able to complete his long journey. He wanted the next thing. He wanted.

He was not supposed to want.

It was not a desired or understood state from where he came from. Wanting meant he was fading.

But want he did. The wants had to be resolved before he could go on.

All he had to do was to say her name. Her real and her othering name. And then he would know. And then the other things would happen. He supposed he was ready. He checked for feelings about that. Feelings. He could not find any.

Self-cleaning accomplished, he whispered to the form suspended in the darkness, "Alais, Juke Joint Johnnie."

"Greetings, Kament. I am here for your report."

Sheryl J. Bize-Boutte is a multidisciplinary writer, poet, and author of four published books. Her latest book, *Betrayal on the Bayou*, is a work of historical fiction that explores the unique and brutal truths of inequality, colorism, and betrayal in the 1800s in the fictional town of Tassin, Louisiana. More about her work at sheryljbize-boutte.com.

ROTTEN

CATEGORY RUNNER UP

The rusted and peeling old Mexican breadbox with the donkey and cactus painting sat abandoned in the shed's corner. Amara's grandmother, Nonny, the old lady with the rotten diabetic legs and fruity breath, had gone to the hospital the night before. Amara's instructions were to "tidy up" the mobile home while her parents awaited the doctors' verdicts. It was annoying to receive instructions at her age, but she supposed her mother's directive was because she was worried about Nonny. Amara had been at it for four hours already, so the house itself was clean. Cleaner than it had been in a long time, based on the dust and grime in the living room. It never crossed Amara's mind to think about how an elderly diabetic woman with bad legs was supposed to clean her home herself.

Amara had found the stash of candy wrappers right away. They were crammed under a thin layer of Kleenex in the box of tissues on the side table. *Twix* appeared to be the favorite, followed by *Snickers* and *Smarties*. Amara crumbled the wrappers in her fingers, and buried them in the trash bag. She'd tell her mother and father later. Her father was right about Nonny. She needed supervision. Amara pursed her lips as she thought of Nonny with her purple lipstick. Why did she wear that lipstick? What was the point? Pappy had been dead for a decade. Amara snorted as she shook her head. Such a foolish old woman.

Amara was certain that Nonny would need to have at least her feet amputated, based on what she had read about untreated diabetic neuropathy earlier in the week. Her mother had not wanted to hear it. Her father, more removed from the situation than her mother, had silently nodded at Amara as she tried to show the *WebMD* web article to her mother. Her mother would have none of it.

Amara reflected on her mother's attitude as she looked around Nonny's home. Mother likes to talk about how independent Nonny used to be. I guess she isn't any more. Getting her care will be expensive. Gritting her teeth, Amara grimaced that the care would take another nickel of her inheritance.

Amara patted the cell phone in her pocket. Her parents would text her when they were ready to pick her up. Fill her in on what was going on. No matter what the doctors would need to do, Nonny would not be returning to live in the mobile home park. She looked around the room at the relics of Nonny's life. Old photos, clay statues Amara herself had made in fourth grade, a partially knitted scarf of red and green, a stack of paperbacks with bookmarks. Junk. All junk. Piles and piles of incomplete things. Like Nonny herself, these things were fragments.

Wiping her forehead, Amara was pleased with the work thus far. The trailer itself was livable. Nothing needed to be saved. She would call the Salvation Army truck in a bit. Amara wandered out to the carport shed to survey the tasks left to complete.

She had piled the useful items to one side already. Gardening tools, watering cans, hedge trimmer, weed whacker, and similar gardening implements reflected the life of a younger, and happier, Nonnie. Amara was turning 40 soon. Her own parents were in their sixties. Nonnie was ageless, but probably closer to 92 than not. She didn't like to talk about her age. She didn't like being reminded that death comes to us all.

Pausing in her stockpiling effort, Amara reflected on the candy wrappers. Who on Earth would bring candy bars to a diabetic old woman? Where did she get them? Mother and Dad did her grocery shopping. Everything was precooked and frozen. All Nonny had to do was microwave the food. Dad took away Nonny's computer and internet access when she started ordering things on Amazon. Things like expensive walnuts and pecans. Dad didn't like her using Facebook either. She had a bad habit of talking online to former coworkers and other relatives. Who knew what she was saying to them? He also took away her cell phone. She didn't have one now, just an old-fashioned landline. Dad also found her address book and took that away, along with her wallet and driver's license. Nonny didn't need to write letters. Taking away her pen and paper had made Nonny cry.

Amara recalled that her mother had reassured Nonny that her family would visit often. Amara frowned a little. *We haven't though, or at least I haven't. I don't have much to say to her. She always used to ask when I was getting married. She just needs to accept that Jack and I don't see a reason to have that ceremony. It is an old-fashioned custom and pointless today.* Amara involuntarily shook her head and dusted off her sweater.

The puzzle of the chocolate bars disturbed Amara, almost as much as the rusting breadbox in the corner. Before long, she had a path cleared to the corner. She grabbed the box and pulled it from its hiding place. She could sort through the things in it as she ate her lunch at the patio table.

Soon she was settled with the open box on the table.

Amara started lifting out the clippings and other contents in the breadbox. They all seemed to be from 1980 to 1985. Amara had been born in April of 1980, but a quick scan of the articles revealed no birth announcement, no pleasant news, and no recipes. All of the articles were about Governor Brown, something called a medfly, a chemical called Malathion, and scribbled notes on a separate piece of paper.

The articles were a hodgepodge of politics, rumors, and horror-mongering. Some of them referred to the medfly as the Bay Area's Three Mile Island. There were several political cartoons, one of which depicted the governor as "Governor Moonbeam" in the form of a giant fly. Another showed him spraying himself in the face with a can labeled "politics". From what she could gather, the governor had suffered from quite a political set-back as a result of his handling of spraying the bugs. She read further into the pile and found small clippings pasted on three by five index cards.

"The medfly's Bay Area infestation was first announced July 8, 1980, after two adult males were found in a suburban San Jose backyard. The news had been deemed so sensitive by pest control specialists that the discovery was kept secret for two weeks as courses of action were discussed "(*Chronicle*, July 30, 1980).

The date and the "suburban San Jose backyard" phrase were circled in pencil with an exclamation in the margin of the card. Amara read through the articles, then hit the one with the most pencil underlines. It was from *The San Jose Mercury News* of July 16, 1981. It read in part:

SAN JOSE, Calif. -- Five helicopters sprayed the pesticide malathion over 10,133 acres today in an escalated aerial attack on the Mediterranean fruit fly which has already caused $4.2 million in produce losses over a three-county zone the state calls a 'major disaster area.'

Gov. Edmund G. Brown Jr. asked President Reagan for federal aid, saying the state's $14 billion agricultural industry faces 'economic disaster' unless it receives help in battling the spreading Medfly infestation. The insect, which so far has hit ripening fruit the hardest, is capable of destroying 200 varieties of fruits and vegetables.

It has not yet spread over a mountain range to the state's big central valleys, heartland of California agriculture. The infestation and quarantine remain confined to a three-county suburban region around the southern shores of San Francisco Bay.

At the bottom of the article, in faint pencil, was a note in Nonny's handwriting. It said, "What have I done?" Amara picked up the separate piece of paper, which was marked, "To be read upon the death of Noella Carreno Lopez". This stated, "I, Noella Carreno Lopez, smuggled an orange from Valencia, Spain on board TWA flight 411 on February 15, 1980. It was meant to be a present for my pregnant daughter. When I unpacked my bag, the orange was covered with white maggots. I threw it in the back yard. Flies showed up after a few days. I am sure now they were medflies. I am certain that I am the person who brought the infestation to California, but I have no way to repay the $4.2 million. However, should I ever develop a fatal illness, I will refuse medication as my punishment for this crime." It was signed Noella Carreno Lopez, August 7, 1982.

"Oh my God! I'm sorry Nonny!" muttered Amara. She bowed her head and wept as her parents pulled in the driveway. She cried for Nonny's rotten foot, her rotten orange, and her rotten life. So many years of guilt, hidden away in a rotting breadbox.

Chris Knoblaugh taught English at the middle school and fifth-grade levels for 18 years at various schools in the San Jose Unified School District before retiring in 2020. She published her first novel in 2018 and released a nonfiction title in 2019. Chris has a BA in English Literature with High College Honors, a B.S. in Biology, and an MA in teaching with reading specialization. Her novels and stories incorporate myths, cryptids, regional traditions, and historical settings. You can find her on Amazon.

Falling to the Middle

Chapter 1

If Kathleen had known that it would be her last appearance in public, she may have given herself a better pep talk. Instead, she whispered to her reflection, "You've got this." Like a cliché. Like a poster with a cat dangling from a tree. Like the mug a miserable worker would use for their morning coffee. Like someone screaming "you've got this" to a drowning person as they treaded water when they needed a life preserver. None of it was helpful.

Kathleen stood in front of the dressing room mirror. "You've got this," she repeated to her reflection. Her hands separated her ponytail in half before she gave the hair a sharp tug to tighten the scrunchie and bring the elastic band closer to her scalp. She rolled her tense shoulders back and down before rotating her neck to work out the kinks in the muscles that seemed to appear out of nowhere in the previous weeks. It could be the series of motel mattresses, or it could be the waning sales that caused the pain. All Kathleen knew was she never had the shoulder problems when her tour started. Soreness in her biceps, tightness in the back of her thighs— those were problems Kathleen knew how to deal with (hot baths and stretching). Sore muscles due to stress were a completely different and new phenomena for her.

At least they let her use the big dressing room. Warm-ups once took place in the offices of the management, with the mall staff asking her for advice while she stretched. Lately, her publicist could only finagle a dressing room in one of the department stores and even then, most were less than ideal. There was the one in Denver, with salespeople constantly knocking on the door to check on her as if Kathleen was a customer. Then there were the darkened rooms of the one in Paramus, New Jersey, in which every other light bulb was turned off to conserve money or energy. At least this store in Tucson gave Kathleen a large, well-lit dressing room. The bulbs worked so well that the bags under Kathleen's eyes could almost cast a shadow over her shoes.

Brighter doesn't mean better, Kathleen thought.

Kathleen began doing jumping jacks, her t-shirt bouncing in a ripple effect on each launch and landing. She wore her "work clothes," a pair of cut-off sweatpants and a t-shirt that had the word "Whatever" written across it. The shirt had seen better days, as had Kathleen, and just like the person wearing it, the shirt was faded but not ready to be tossed aside yet. Kathleen wore her dirtiest tennis shoes and had fixed her hair to ensure her brown roots showed through her blond bangs. She needed the audience to always know that she was one of them. And to be one of them, she had to show she didn't have time to get her hair colored or the money to buy expensive workout clothes.

A knock on the fitting room door stopped her jumping. "It's time," a voice informed her from the other side.

Kathleen unlocked the door to see her assistant/ publicist/ friend Melissa Davis standing there, hands clutching the clipboard their kids had decorated, her curly hair pulled up into a messy bun on top of her head. When Kathleen had mentioned that she would look more professional in nice slacks, Melissa bought a black blazer and some button-down shirts instead. There had been a time when Melissa would take Kathleen's advice, a time when she would immediately hit the women's section of the store to pick out a pair of pants that she knew Kathleen would approve of. Now Kathleen had to be satisfied with the fact that the shirt had at least been ironed in the motel room that they shared.

"Are you ready to head down?"

Kathleen proceeded to jump in place a few times, her head going back and forth to both shoulders like a human metronome. After a few seconds of bouncing in place, Kathleen announced, "I'm ready."

As the pair weaved through the junior's department towards the elevator, Kathleen asked her usual question. "How's the crowd?"

Melissa's lips curled down. "Honestly? A little sparse."

The pair rode the elevator down, Melissa taking the step behind Kathleen's and towering over her. "Like Wichita sparse? Or like Madison sparse?" Kathleen turned and checked out her ponytail in the mirrored glass in the elevator.

"More like Cheyenne," Melissa answered. "But maybe when they see you, they'll come over."

Kathleen shot Melissa a look. "Yeah, right. Like they happened to be at the mall buying a sweater but wait! There's that fitness lady, Marge! Let's put our bags down and workout for a bit." Kathleen rolled her eyes as the elevator brought them to the ground floor. "Get real."

Kathleen stepped out of the elevator first.

"I am real," Melissa grumbled.

Women mixed among displays of shoes and handbags, focused on the products in front of them. Behind one of the cosmetic counters, two employees wearing lab coats waved to the pair as they walked by. "Hey there, Kathleen!" one yelled as they passed. Several people at her counter turned to look to see where her comment was directed. Kathleen's mouth immediately went into a smile as she flexed her right arm and shouted, "Stay stronger, ladies!" One of the women cheered and clapped, in approval of Kathleen's shouting her catch phrase.

Kathleen's smile disappeared as they walked into the mall and to Kathleen's shock, she noticed just how small the set up was for her promotion. There was a "backstage" as Melissa always requested but it couldn't have been more than six feet long, barely enough to stretch inside of. The head of the mall security parted the dark fabric that blocked the small area, letting the women in. The events coordinator from the mall had been prepping a table next to the stage with black markers and the headshots Melissa had provided him. As Kathleen entered the backstage area, Melissa stayed out to help set up books at the table.

Kathleen raised her arms to shoulder height and twisted her body. She almost swatted the security guard as he approached her from behind.

"My wife was a huge fan," the security guard said, his arms folded over his chest.

The past tense in that sentence didn't elude Kathleen. "That's great. I really appreciate it." Kathleen motioned to a box containing copies of her book. "I can sign one of those for her, if you want me to."

"Oh, that's okay," the guard said, his hand dismissing the offer. "She may already own it. But thanks anyway."

Kathleen gave him a wafer-thin grin. Melissa and the man from the mall had joined them in the staging area. The event coordinator, a middle-aged man in a suit too large for his frame, went over the plan one more time with Melissa, ignoring Kathleen. "That time limit is strict. Do you hear me? We need our men to disassemble everything and be out of here before I have to pay overtime." Melissa nodded and confirmed. As he walked off with the security guard, Melissa whispered, "I hate when they treat me like I am stupid."

Kathleen ignored her. "It doesn't sound like too many people are out there."

"It's fine," Melissa said. When Kathleen shot her a look, she repeated it. "It's fine."

"Just go introduce me so bad suit doesn't yell at us for going over when the crowd lingers to talk to me." Melissa walked out of the area, with the squeak of a microphone informing Kathleen that everything was starting.

"I want to thank you all for coming out here to get fit with someone who believes you are already strong and knows that you can STAY STRONGER!" Melissa always shouted that last part; she almost blew out the speakers. Once upon a time, Melissa shouted to be heard over Kathleen's supporters, but what followed was a sprinkling of light applause. One lone "woo!" joined in the clapping.

Melissa continued her introduction as Kathleen walked close to the curtain's opening, ready to make her entrance. She smoothed her bangs with her hand. "And after some invigorating cardio, Kathleen will be sticking around to sign copies of her new Eating to Stay Stronger, Ladies! book, which includes meal ideas and fitness charts so you can track the progress she knows you can make. And without further ado, here she is… Kathleen Baresi!"

Kathleen ran around the curtain and leapt onto the dais, ending with her arms extended as if she just dismounted from the double parallel bars at the Olympics. The choice to leap and not to use the steps was always a crowd pleaser and a signature move of Kathleen's. "How's it going Tuscon?!" Her voice didn't need a microphone.

Stacy Ryan is a writer whose personal narrative pieces have been published in online parenting magazines and on storytelling websites. She is currently working on *Falling to the Middle*, a novel about the messy and fun parts between the beginning and the end of life. You can find her at stacyryanwrites.com.

48 STATES

LIBRARY OF CONGRESS

ONLINE RESOURCES DIVISION

DATE: Received to Archive October 1, 2043

October 15, 2040

NOTICE TO EVACUATE

North Dakota

YOU ARE HEREBY NOTIFIED THAT THIS AREA IS NOW UNDER THE JURISDICTION OF THE DEPARTMENT OF ENERGY AS DIRECTED BY PRESIDENTIAL EXECUTIVE ORDER.

ALL CIVILIANS MUST EVACUATE THE AREA WITHIN 30 DAYS. TUNE YOUR RADIOS TO AM 1040 OR VISIT WWW.ENERGY TERRITORY//EVACUATION.GOV FOR FURTHER INSTRUCTIONS.

<u>Chapter 1</u>

Twenty pairs of eyes followed River as she entered the bar. She tracked them out of the corner of her eye as she walked towards an open seat, never acknowledging their scrutiny. A sigh of relief escaped her lips as she eased herself on to one of the barstools. She'd been up and down the highway a dozen times in her rig, with nothing but natural gas flares for company. Up and back again until her arms ached from dragging the hoses in and out of the holding tanks. Another night without an injury, and more overtime pay in her bank account.

A bar back placed a bowl of freshly made popcorn in front of her. The buttery aroma transported her back to her childhood when jump ropes and sleepovers ruled the day…*Eeny, meeny, miny, moe, catch a tiger by the toe, if he hollers, let him go, eeny, meeny, miny, moe, my mother told me to pick the very best one…* A delivery from the bartender brought her back to the present.

"This is for you," he said, placing a glass of what was likely tequila—men always sent that, or Jägermeister—in front of her.

"Send it back, Bobby," River said, pushing the drink away.

"Sure thing," he said. "If I were you, I would skip the drink and get out. Most of these guys just got back in town from their shifts."

"Thanks for the warning," River said. "I've had a long night myself, so please just bring me my usual?"

River watched Bobby walk away to make her drink. If she'd been looking for a lover, he would have been a good choice with his tight black T-shirts and full sleeves of ink. His right arm was a mix of multi-colored peacocks with gleaming feathers, mermaids and the rings of Saturn posted mid-bicep. An elaborately inked treasure map covered the other arm, but he never revealed what the prize was. A nose ring dangled from his septum, giving him a menacing air, but she knew it was all a show. He'd come to nurse a broken heart. She wasn't sure of the particulars, only that he preferred being in the Territory to San Francisco. River reminded him how crazy it was to leave California for such a rotten, dangerous place, but he just laughed and told her "Anywhere can go rotten if you fuck it up bad enough." She'd nod in agreement, knowing only too well that he was right.

"You're being stubborn, as usual," Bobby said as he returned with her rum and coke. "I'm going to say it again. Most of these guys just got off their twenty and are ready to party."

She knew what he meant. Williston, North Dakota served as the main outpost for the Territory. The state had been emptied by forced evacuation and then repopulated with a mix of workers, mostly veterans from the Caliphate War, working on rig crews in twenty-day shifts or hitches. As soon as the shifts ended, the crews came back into town ready to make up for lost time. If you wanted to have a drink and mind your own business, you patronized Outerlands. The other ten or so bars catered to a mix of preferences and price points. With a 20:5 ratio of men to women, River knew Bobby was reminding her to be careful. Women were usually meant for one thing inside the Territory, and it wasn't for hauling.

Still, she was always glad to see the neon sign for Outerlands as she came around the bend in her rig on Highway 85. Its grey concrete floors were worn and pockmarked from years of use. The wood-paneled walls and lack of windows made it dark inside. But the drinks were strong, and the management favored music from the 1970s. She chose Outerlands because she liked the name, and because they held a trivia night once a month. A voracious reader, she was good at collecting random bits of information, and usually managed to win a few rounds, especially if the topics involved history and literature. She wasn't in the mood to be chased out of her only source of entertainment.

"I can handle myself," River said.

"Maybe," he said. "But I feel compelled to ask for what must be the one hundredth time, why don't you get the hell out of here already?"

"And leave all this behind?" River mocked. "Compared to being stationed in France, this is paradise."

For nearly two years she'd managed to avoid telling him the truth. That her husband had killed himself and left her with a mound of debt and few options except to leave her daughter and work in this God-forsaken wasteland. That at eighty dollars an hour–more than one hundred if she worked overtime–she'd signed the contract to drive a haul truck inside the Territory as soon as they'd offered her a position.

"You know you don't belong here with all these *heathens*," Bobby said.

"*Heathens*…That's pretty good," River replied. "Your Berkeley roots are showing. Are you referring to their lack of godliness or just a general barbarous nature?"

"Both, and for the record, it was Berkeley undergrad. I studied creative writing at the University of San Francisco," Bobby said. "Until my scholarship ran out. The government cancelled student loans for MFA programs around the time they issued the first list of banned books."

"Here's to words and their meanings," River said, remembering that day. Her mother, a librarian, was outraged that the government ordered books it considered subversive to be pulled from the shelves. A sensation of someone standing behind her pulled River back to the present. She began to breathe through her mouth to avoid the stench of body odor and solvents that hung in the air as he leaned in to speak to her.

"What's the matter?" he asked. "Don't you like my gift? Maybe I should have sent you what I'm having. Bartender! Bring over another 'Taste of a Woman.'"

"No thanks," River said, wanting nothing to do with the bourbon cocktail he was pushing. "I'm not drinking."

"That's a bunch of bullshit," he said, cutting her off. "I see your glass right there."

"You didn't let me finish," River said. "I was about to say I'm not drinking with other people."

"Well that is too bad," he said. "Because I've decided you and I are going to have ourselves a little party tonight."

"That's not going to happen," River said, keeping her gaze straight ahead.

"Oh, come on," he said. "I can be a lot of fun."

"Actually, I was just leaving."

"We can walk out together then," he said. "Are we clear?"

The majority of the bar patrons, never candidates for charm school to begin with, sensed the promise of violence and turned to watch. Her unwanted visitor grinned, egged on by the spectators, revealing a mouth full of missing and half-broken teeth.

"I promise to be nice," he said, grabbing River's newly cropped brown hair. The pain was immediate as he dragged her closer to his rank breath. "Don't make this harder than it has to be. I don't want to have to hurt you."

River nodded as she rose from the barstool. Quickly, she stomped on his foot, grabbed his other hand, and brought his arm in close, using it as a fulcrum to send him tumbling. The man let out a whimper as his bone snapped. He landed flat on his back with a thud. River snatched her Glock from the back of her jeans and pointed it straight at his chest.

"If you so much as raise a finger, I will put a bullet through your heart before you can get off the ground," River said. "Are we clear?"

Evette Davis is the author of *48 States*, as well as the *Dark Horse Trilogy*. She founded Flesh & Bone, an independent publishing imprint in 2014. Her work has been published in the *San Francisco Chronicle* and *Book Country*. Along with writing, she co-owns a public affairs firm based in San Francisco. For more on Evette and her writing endeavors, check out evettedavis.com.

Last Sunrise

From the inside of the dryer, Dani nudged open the door and peeked into the laundromat that she'd called home for the past four nights. She knew she was pushing it staying in the same place for that long, but she felt safer somehow cradled inside the steel drum. And it was warmer than trying to curl up in some alleyway between old brick buildings in Cleveland Heights. Besides, Leon would never dream to look for her in here. Stupid prick. He could keep her dead brother's fucking necklace for all she cared. No matter how many tricks she turned in a day, she would never earn enough to get it back anyway. He kept moving the finish line. She never wanted to see his mean, pockmarked face ever again. His attempt at growing a goatee did nothing to improve his ugly mug. When she'd mentioned that, he'd tattooed her jaw with his cheap garnet pinky ring. Absentmindedly, she rubbed the still-tender spot, all senses on high alert as she scanned the detergent-scented room for signs of life. Certainly smelled better than an alley in here. Kinda reminded her of her mom's laundry room. She shook her head, rattling the memory from her brain. She couldn't afford to get sentimental now. No place for mushy shit in her game.

Unfolding her skinny legs, she stepped backward onto the linoleum and stuffed a ratty, threadbare blanket into her backpack. She tiptoed into the washroom and locked the flimsy particleboard door behind her. Catching sight of herself in the mirror, she flinched. She plucked at jagged strands of knife-shorn, Clairol number 2 black hair, focusing on the amber circles under her bloodshot eyes. Her cheekbones and lips, which one old girlfriend used to call ripe apples and juicy oranges, were now bony and chapped. She turned on the water, freezing her face awake with a splash. Rinsing her mouth, she spit traces of pink into the sink. She unzipped the front pocket of her backpack, retrieving a small burner phone that glowed green in the dim light.

January 20th, 2008–5:36 am.

"Happy 18th, freakshow," she mumbled, pressing the shut off button to conserve the dwindling battery. Slipping the phone back into the pocket, she felt a piece of forgotten paper. Crumpling it, she muttered, "That'll never happen," as she tossed the persistent AA lady's contact information into the trash. She stuffed sweatshirted arms into a fleecy denim jacket and crept out the broken back door. Tugging the straps of the backpack tighter, Dani moved in the dark morning toward the street, icy wind biting her face, stinging her watering eyes. At the corner, a cab idled in front of an all-night diner, foggy exhaust pluming around the trunk. She opened the back door and blew in with the wind, plunking down on the grimy seat.

"Where to?," the driver asked, wrinkling his nose.

"3333 Chadbourne. Shaker"

"Fare's twenty bucks. You got money?"

Her steely eyes met his in the rear view.

"I got money."

"Show me."

"Fuck you," she said, kicking open the door.

"Take a bath, dirtbag, you stink!"

She stuck both middle fingers high in the air and began to walk the three miles to Shaker Heights. Just one of the old lady's rings and she'd be good to go. No scoring this time, her waning conscience scolded. The money had to last a few weeks. Headlights swept the pavement from behind, and Dani spun around, sticking out her thumb. The car made a wide berth around her, speeding away. Pulling her collar snug around her neck, she picked up her pace.

Two more hours till sunrise.

If she'd known that this one would be her last, she might have used the remaining battery to call her ex and tell her she loved her. She might have called her mother to say she was sorry. Or, she just might have turned back around and called the AA lady, who probably would have bought her breakfast at the diner, maybe talked to her about treatment, or offered her a place to shower.

But Dani walked on, her stride determined.

Leon waited in the dark street outside her childhood home with a loaded Glock on his lap. His car was warm. He fingered the thick gold chain around his neck and waited.

Kellyn Liston is a US Navy aviation veteran and advocate of all beings, especially the marginalized. In Our Blood is her debut novel about generational trauma and the power of the human spirit, soon to be self-published. She lives on her native Florida Gulf Coast. Find her at kellynliston.com.

THE BECKONING

I.

Jemima didn't know when exactly the figure had appeared. One day she was sure—pretty sure, at least—that there had been nothing unusual about the idyllic forest scene she had selected as the background photo of her new iPhone. A few weeks later she realized a small black shape was frozen in the frame in the distance, its hand reaching towards her as if mid-greeting.

She had been surprised but, since the figure was there, she thought it must have been there the whole time and somehow she'd just missed it. Of course she would not have selected that particular image as her background photo if she *had* seen the figure in the photo. But, the shape was there so that, she assumed, was that.

The photo was from Cranston, Rhode Island, not too far south from Providence. She had spent a few exhausted days there on her East Coast train trip with Jake before Jake had realized he needed some time for himself and moved out of their apartment in the armpit of Boston.

But that weekend, they had wandered around the forest, their feet sinking into the floor of the woods carpeted with mulch and fallen leaves as the wind rustled the treetops and bent them over the path they walked on. The air had smelled green, and fresh, and the tiniest bit chilly, like the first draft of air moved by the opening of a fridge door, even if Jemima had to admit it had also felt isolated and pretty creepy.

She had taken more photos than she usually did: it was her and Jake's first trip together and she had been determined to collect memories along the journey. Truthfully, she had also thought what a nice Christmas card it would make: some shots of the two adventurers exploring the world. She had the whole look and feel of the photos planned out: the two of them in casual clothes, hoodies and woolen hats and hiking boots, red apples in their cheeks and grins on their faces. Yes, the photos would make a good, if cheesy, card.

She had paid extra care and attention to the framing of the shots she took, making sure neither of them sported a double chin or an unflattering mid-photo blink. She had even grabbed a few candid shots of Jake as he surveyed the woodlands with the air of a Puritan settler selecting a spot for his cabin. There was something distinguished about his profile in the photo, the strong jaw covered with stubble and the nose a straight, forward-looking intent.

But then Jake had broken up with her anyway and Jemima hadn't sent any cards.

Now, Jemima stared at the photo of the stretch of path that the branches with the yellow and orange and green leaves closed over so that it looked more like a dark tunnel that plunged into the depths of the woods than just a path through it, and the black shape that stood at the end of it.

How strange: for the life of her, she could not remember anyone else in the woods that day.

She did recall Jake standing just a foot or two to the side; so close, in fact, that she had snapped the shot when he had leant towards her to give her the quickest, most fleeting of kisses on her cheek, and she had thought—she'd had the nerve to think—*finally*, here was her chance to take one photo without the constant presence of her boyfriend.

Would he still have broken up with her if she had not had that thought?

The question materialized from thin air, it seemed, and Jemima swallowed the lump of follow-up material that was sure to make an appearance: if it wasn't for that, then it would have been because she was fat, and stupid, and naive, and sexually unadventurous.

And now, also, apparently going crazy. Or just blind?

Jemima peered at the photo, trying to make out more details of the figure. The hand that was reaching towards her was large-ish, certainly bigger than her own hands. So, a man? The shoulder that the arm connected to also looked broad and there was a vague, triangular impression to the overall shape of the body.

So: a man.

But who?

Jemima pinched and spread her fingers on the screen to zoom in closer on the photo. What a strange thing to have photographed, however accidentally! For, as she kept straining her eyes to make out more details of the figure at the end of the path she could have sworn that something about the man's attitude—*shifted*: when she first became aware of it she had thought it looked as if the man was waving at her, just another hiker wandering in the woods of an autumnal day.

But now: now, it almost looked like the shape was *beckoning* to her.

The thought dropped into her head and Jemima found herself unable to shake it loose again. For the hand of the figure was quite clearly no longer showing her the palm, as you might if you were casually greeting some stranger you encountered on a hike on a sunny day. Now it very much looked as if it was showing her the back of the hand, the fingers curled behind, as if to say *"come with me."*

But that *was* crazy, surely.

It was more likely that the figure had been that way all along and she had just interpreted the indistinct shape of the hand as a greeting. That must be it: a photograph from four months ago doesn't just change on its own.

Jemima put her phone on her desk, screen side down so she would not have to look at it anymore, and went to cook some noodles for her dinner.

II.

After a meager dinner Jemima got changed into her jogging bottoms and trainers to head out for her daily run. She hated running, and always had, but the thought of bumping into Jake on campus or in any of the bars they both used to frequent with her muffin top bulging out of her black skinny jeans got shivers like pearls of ice sliding down her spine. How could she make Jake realize what he was missing if there was that treacherous, warm roll of flesh betraying the best intentions of her clothes to contain it?

And so she changed into her sporty clothes and got ready to go for a run.

She picked up her phone. And almost dropped it.

The black shape in the photo that had been lurking somewhere in the background with its arm extended towards her was now noticeably bigger: it was easily the height of Jemima's thumb and she could see details that she had not been able to make out earlier: the suggestion of a hat on the head of the figure, or the *man* (for it was now quite clear to Jemima that it was, indeed, a man with a chiseled chin and slightly indented cheeks with the shadow of a beard growing in) and the right leg was bent at the knee as if the man had been caught in the middle of the act of taking a step towards her. Had he previously not been standing still at the back edge of the photo, surprised by the photographer who had snuck upon him and ensnared him into the shot?

Jemima shook her head as if to force the man to retreat into the depths of the tunnel that led further into the heart of the forest. Then she closed her eyes and counted to five, and with a deep breath she had learned to take and release in her yoga class she opened her eyes and looked at the screen of her phone again.

Jemima thought she would have screamed if she had any breath left in her chest but it had all leaked out as her brain tried its best to make sense of what she was looking at. She ended up falling hard on her bum in the chair in front of the desk, her gaze glued to the man in the photo.

He was now looking straight at her, as if all along he had been traveling through time and distance to rush those last few feet towards her and then— what? What would happen when the man reached the edge of the screen?

Would he tumble out? Or would he press his face against the screen and scratch and strike at the glass as if to break it from the inside?

This is crazy, Jemima thought, monkeys juggling the loose marbles of her mind on rollerskates type of fucking crazy. She put her phone down again, trapping—as she thought—the man in the sliver of space that existed between her desk and the screen of the phone.

Then she leant her face in her hands and was relieved to find the tears trailing down her cheeks already.

Heidi Marjamäki hails from Vaasa, Finland, but studied literature in Scotland and worked in Oxford and London before making her home in Berlin. She works in a tech startup as product lead and is currently working on her first novel. You can find her at heidiwritesthings.com.

THE BEGINNING

French Quarter, New Orleans. Present day.

An invisible line runs around the perimeter of the Vieux Carré, only discernible to those who bother to look closely. And only to those who have the gift of seeing past the ordinary. It's said the border line was cast by a powerful priestess who vowed to protect her children and keep their treasured city safe from the darkness that stole her beloved husband and sought to absorb and wield the power of those innocents who are graced with the light. Over time, the stories of the darkness have been forgotten as its power diminished, and the shimmer of the border line has faded as the city has forgotten its existence and purpose, but there are still some who remember, and who can even now sense the growing shadow threatening to once again bring destruction and death as the power of the border line weakens.

"I'll walk from here." Ariella Domingue paid the cab driver and jumped out of the backseat before he could protest. She slung her faded black leather backpack over one shoulder and hefted her oversized duffel, then walked slowly down the old street at the edge of the Vieux Carré, now known as the French Quarter, until she crossed over into the heart of the city. She felt a tremor of fear and excitement course through her as she stepped back into the world that had been the true home of her childhood, and then she straightened her spine and headed to the center of it all.

In this oldest part of New Orleans, sidewalks were badly cracked and sometimes disappeared altogether, and the street was riddled with potholes. The stench of rotting garbage mingled with the smell of the ancient city sewers and with car exhaust as drivers inched slowly down the one way street, narrowly missing oversized garbage bag falling of the curbs on the edge of the street. It should have repelled her. The mess, and the grime, and the smells all often did scare away a lot of would be tourists, yet she looked beyond all of that and felt the welcoming pull of finally coming home.

She listened hard, and saw more, saw deeper. There was a lone coronet playing a soulful rendition of Amazing Grace and it filtered down from one of the many banquettes that overlooked the street. The music settled over her like a balm to her homesick soul, and the decay and rubble could not hide the soul of the city. She'd missed it all more than she'd even realized, and it was as if a light turned back on inside her. She could almost feel the click, and then the magic rushed back, filling her up. That light of that magic had been off for far too long, so long she hadn't realized how dark her world had become, but it came flooding back now, filling her down to the tips of her fingers and ends of her toes until they tingled with it. She soaked it in, unsure how to handle the rush of it all, and looked around once more, saw beyond her first impressions, glimpsed the secret courtyards lush with green plants and saw the hidden spaces. She breathed in the smell of the earthy humidity and colorful blooming flowers, heard the cascade of water pouring from fountains. The aroma of a Cajun mirepoix, that holy trinity of onion, celery, and bell peppers, sizzled and steamed out the back door of a kitchen restaurant in an alleyway. It would go into gumbo, or étouffée or maybe jambalaya, or any number of other regional favorites, she knew. How long had it been since she'd had a true New Orleans meal? Tonight, she promised herself. For now, she needed to find her way to the church before she made her way to her aunt's home. She had a promise to keep, and it had been waiting for 16 years.

She walked further down the cobbled street towards the infamous Jackson Square. It was also where the St. Louis Cathedral towered over the city, and called both the wicked and the weary into its cool sanctuary in search of answers. Once, Ari had been a believer, in occasional attendance when her performing duties allowed it, especially during the big holidays like Christmas and All Souls Day. She still remembered the sharp, pungent smell of the smoky incense layered over the scent of melting candle wax, and wished with sudden intense longing to be 10 years old again, dressed in her best Sunday dress and sandwiched between her aunt and uncle in the overfilled cathedral at Christmas. It was a time when hundreds of strangers gathered together to sing Christmas carols and find a moment of peace, and for those few precious moments, everything in the world was just right. The vision wavered and then disappeared into the tattered remnants of Ari's memories, but it was a good solid reminder of a better, simpler time in her life, before everything had changed and ended.

At the edge of Jackson Square she rested her duffel on the curb and took in the crowds of tourists, the entertainers that ranged from artists peddling their creations, to musicians performing the city's favorite jazz songs, to the fortune tellers who slyly offered hope for a better future for just a few coins and bills. And then her attention was snagged by a girl of no more than 10 years old, dressed plainly in jeans just a little too short, and a frayed gray t-shirt that had seen more than its share of washes. The girl's cap was pulled low over dark curling hair caught through the back, and Ari was reminded of herself at that age. Her eyes narrowed when she watched the girl nimbly reach into an oblivious tourist's oversized purse, then saw her unerringly pull out a wallet before dropping it into her own dark bag. The girl had skills, and if Ari hadn't known what to look for, she'd never have noticed the young thief casually working her way through the crowd. She counted four more takes before the girl got herself into trouble. A man walked up behind the girl just as she pulled a red wallet from a woman's purse and dropped it into her own bag. The man grabbed her arm. From Ari's distant viewpoint, she couldn't hear the conversation, but the man still had hold of the girl's wrist and appeared to be making angry gestures and looking around, probably for a cop, while the girl glanced around wildly, seeking a way out.

Without thinking, Ari scooped up her things and strode over to the girl and man.

"Bella! I thought I told you to head to the car! We still need to pack up the rest of our things!" Ari said loudly, coming up behind the young girl. The girl's eyes widened when she realized Ari was speaking to her, but she only watched as Ari rounded on the man and took in the scene. Then she launched into the man.

"What is going on here? Sir, get your hands off my daughter. Bella, do you know this man?" Ari demanded. The girl mutely shook her head, trying to figure out what was going on, but smart enough to know to play along.

The man looked angry. "Just one minute, this girl was trying to steal from my wife!" He accused. "I saw her reach into her bag and pull out her wallet just seconds ago!" The man was fuming, and his wife stood beside him, looking confused.

"I beg your pardon sir, but you must be mistaken. My daughter was just walking to the car after our long theater performance today, and would never do something like that!" The girl was looking pale but defiant, and Ari turned to the man's wife. "Ma'am, you can easily placate your husband. Is your wallet missing?" Ari asked her.

At that moment, the young girl swallowed visibly, and Ari reached out to put what appeared to be a motherly hand on her shoulder, stopping the girl before she could run, while the man's wife opened her purse, still unaware of what had just happened. She stared at her husband, then looked at Ari and the young girl.

"I'm so sorry, my husband must have been mistaken." And with that, the woman pulled out a red wallet from just inside her purse.

Michelle M. Gates writes compelling character driven fiction with strong female protagonists and a touch of magical realism, in addition to her other writing endeavors. Her current novel in progress centers around an out of work theater performer who returns to New Orleans seeking answers to her own lost past while getting thrown into a quest to save her beloved city from a curse centuries in the making. When she's not writing, you can find Michelle fueling her coffee obsession, baking profusely, and dreaming about her next travel destination while chasing her kids. Find her online at MichelleMGates.com.

THE INTERIM SOLUTION

July, Chicago

Emma wondered if she was starting to slip. That's the thing about being crazy. You don't know if you're sliding into the hell of another episode, or if you're just having a bad day. Which this was shaping up to be. The one thing she did know was this meeting was important to Tom.

Emma and Tom Lewis walked past the final two shops — the dry cleaner and the pet store. Emma checked their reflections. She looked good, walking next to her handsome husband, with his lean physique. He wore a well-tailored jacket and jeans that fit just right. She had chosen to wear a shirt in Tom's favorite shade of blue, and slacks that hid her recent weight gain.

When they met at UChicago, Tom had loved her curvy figure and wavy brown hair. Now he didn't like those curves as much as he used to. She wasn't really fat, just a few extra pounds. And today, Emma had spent extra time on her makeup, she didn't want Pastor Jason to notice anything unusual. Tom's arm placed over Emma's shoulder presented an image of a happy couple, just the right kind of people for Pastor Jason's special church.

Tom looked over. "Honey, Pastor Jason will get us over this rough patch. He helps lots of people. The Henrys are happy now." The Henrys acted so happy they scared Emma. Except that Mrs. Henry was fooling around with some teacher at the junior college; everyone in town knew but the pastor, Tom, and Mr. Henry. Emma enjoyed that the church didn't know *everything* that happened in the neighborhood – they weren't that good.

They arrived at the shop and Emma rang the bell. The church moved after months of searching for suitable property. The good-sized toy and candy store was an improvement over the previous location. She'd visited the store as a child and loved wandering among the toys and books.

Emma thought again that it was surprising the church could afford a new space. She'd always considered Pastor's ability to create guilt lucrative, this seemed proof.

Pastor smiled as he opened the door. "Welcome to our new home. My office is in back."

He was a vision of slick, teeth to toes — everything shone. His shoes and belt were crocodile, his tan slacks had a razor's edge crease. His round cheeks flushed with pride. Emma noted he'd dyed his hair dark brown again, covering the grey.

As they followed him to the back of the store, Emma recalled how it had looked and smelled when she was small. The candy racks had been in the front, along the walls had been toys, dolls, books, and games. The racks and shelves now held religious tracts and Bibles.

They entered the beige kitchen with cheap appliances and a freshly polished floor. Emma thought the man matched the kitchen, shiny without much substance. Pastor clicked on the coffee maker and placed a creamer from the fridge on the table, next to a matching sugar bowl. Spoons rested on folded white napkins before three of the chairs.

Pastor said, "Mrs. Hill had a meeting, but fixed snacks before she left. I'm blessed to have a wonderful woman like her in my life. Besides her efforts to support my goals, she always allocates time to assist members in need."

Tom nodded appreciatively. "You're a lucky man. We appreciate her help."

As they settled at the table, Emma wondered if Mrs. Hill was well paid for her efforts, since she seemed to do more work than anyone else. Once seated, Pastor Jason reached for a plate of cookies from the counter and set it between Tom and himself. Tom took a cookie, broke it in half, and then snapped each half in half. He looked expectantly at Pastor Jason.

Pastor began, "Emma, I understand that you have been having trouble at home. Let me help. Your family should stay together. It is the Lord's way. Tom, a little discipline is fine, but I don't like seeing bruises."

Emma had thought they were hidden under her make-up. It's hard to hide purple, but she'd recently found a good product online. Tom expected flawless. Sensing this was going nowhere good any time soon, Emma focused on her nails. She realized they needed a manicure and hoped no one would notice. She studied the table and thought a cookie would ease her discomfort.

She was about to ask for one when Pastor Jason said loudly, "I said, Emma, please pour some coffee." She served in order — Pastor's, Tom's, and then her own. She wedged the pot into place and returned to her seat.

Emma looked at her husband. His brown hair shone in a sunbeam, and the graying temples made his blue eyes sparkle. She tried to get his attention to convey that she cared and wanted to save their marriage. She missed the kind, gentle man he once was, and she hoped he would be again. But Tom looked at his cookie, his coffee, and his pastor. With a sigh, Emma glanced over her cup at Pastor Jason; their eyes met.

"You look run down, dear," he said. "I'm worried. In fact, I discussed you today with Dr. Dawes. If you cannot take care of your husband and kids, you should go back to Mercy. We'll arrange it with their team so you can work with Dr. Dawes."

Tom reached over, took her hand, and smiled. He said, "You'll remember Dr. Dawes. He's a new leader in our church. Honey, you know it's not good when you get depressed and don't take care of yourself or the family. You're not dressing like you used to…"

Pastor Jason interrupted, "Tom, if you didn't like what Emma was wearing, you should have said something before you left the house. If Emma needs housekeeping and fashion refresher courses, that's a different conversation. We'll send her to the women's group. They can be such a help when people get confused."

Emma didn't want another doctor, didn't want any refresher courses, and certainly didn't want a makeover at some church-sanctioned salon. She wasn't sure what was going on and caught the men glancing at each other. There was no easy way to say no, but anything would be an improvement over this current hell. "Fine, if you think it will help," Emma said with a gentle sigh.

Pastor Jason steepled his hands. "I'll have Rhonda coordinate. Emma, you'll go for an update. That'll make Tom happy, and you'll feel better."

"Pastor, thank you so much," Tom said. "The sitter will stay late. The girls can make a day of it. Honey, doesn't that sound like fun?"

She looked up and smiled at her husband, hoping this effort might save the marriage and turn him back into the man who once had loved her.

Pastor Jason didn't seem convinced by her smile. "Emma, you have to try. We've been patient with your ups and downs, but you need to step up and get better. It's taking too long. We want you to get on with your life. If you don't take your responsibilities as a wife and mother seriously, the church will have to intervene. Let's pray and ask the Lord to heal Emma."

October, San Francisco

In her office, Ann Dorchester stood, stretched, and looked down at the San Francisco Bay. Her success in mergers and acquisitions earned a corner spot with an expansive view. She loved watching the fog slip under the Golden Gate Bridge as the 2:30PM Sausalito ferry motored to the dock.

Ann walked to the closet and opened its mirrored door to check her look. Her natural blond hair was courtesy of the best stylist in town, house calls every three weeks. She liked the way her clothes hung on her model's figure, thanks to the lean genes that ran in the family.

The phone rang. Ann returned to her desk, settled in her Aeron chair, and hit the speaker button. She wished she was tech comfortable enough to edit complex agreements online, but she still needed hard copy for some projects, like today's. She slid a fat folder over and started talking.

Two hours of tough negotiation later, she'd moved the opposing sides closer. The sale of the building on Sansome would close soon. Real estate wasn't Ann's usual work, and she'd enjoyed learning a new topic to help one of her colleagues. Her latest uncomfortable designer shoes were stuck together under the desk where she'd kicked them during the call. She reached with her foot and could only find one shoe. With a sigh, she pushed back her chair and crawled under the desk, as her assistant, Bob Wright, tapped on the door and entered.

"Ann," he said with a smile, "Did you lose your shoes under your desk again?"

"Of course I did." She laughed as she returned to her chair and straightened her jacket.

E. Coyle Divers works in technology. Her fiction is about complex and dangerous relationships between friends, families, and colleagues. Occasional criminal acts, even a murder or two, have appeared in her pages. She finds inspiration on public transit or while cycling around cities in the USA and Europe. You can reach her at ecdsf11@gmail.com.

Tiger in the Night

Screams battered the muggy evening air. Pepper Nyx straightened from her lean against the open door of Turtle Creek Coffee. She nudged a cinder block into place with her foot to keep herself from getting locked out and stepped away from the brick building. The setting sun sent streaks of fire into her eyes as she searched for the commotion, and she lifted a hand to shade her eyes. Along the far edge of the parking lot was a lone car where a tall man was arguing with a woman. The first shots of adrenaline sent her heart fluttering against her ribs and leached the moisture out of her mouth. Inhaling sharply, she fished under her apron for her phone as she shouted back into the coffee shop kitchen.

"Abby, if I'm not back in two minutes, call the police!"

"Pepper?" the older woman at the sink called back. "Pepper, what's going on?"

Pepper was already headed across the lot. Her grip tightened on her phone until the case creaked in protest as she forced her breathing back under her control. Her worn black sneakers ground the gravel into the asphalt with every hurried step.

"Let go of me!" a woman shouted. Pepper slowed, picking her way by looking through the phone's camera. She fumbled for the video setting as the sound of a low growl seemed to surround the entire lot. The tall man had his back to her, pinning the woman against the side of a car. Pepper couldn't tell if he was trying to get the door open or if he was grabbing at the woman herself. The poor woman was frantically shoving at him, kicking him in the legs and beating him with her purse, but he didn't seem to notice.

"Hey!" Pepper punched the air out of her belly to make the sound carry, finally getting her phone to start recording. The man looked over his shoulder and Pepper smiled her most sweetly dangerous smile. "That's right, scumbag. Show me your face."

"Call the police!" the woman cried, still fighting to get the man off of her.

"My boss already did," Pepper said calmly, though her heart was racing. She moved around toward the front of the vehicle to get a better angle on the attacker's face. "I'm just going to get a nice close-up of this dirtbag. I'm sure the police are going to be very excited for this debut. Or maybe this isn't your first time on screen," she taunted the attacker. Slowly, he turned toward her. Her stomach churned with fear and fury, but she kept the phone steady. "Maybe they've seen you before. I bet this is the only way you get womanly attention, isn't it, tough guy?"

Pepper ground parking lot grit under the toe of her shoe to relieve the urge to run. She had the distinct impression that she was baiting something dangerous, something primal, and it made her feel overly caffeinated. The man's face should have been handsome, with a strong jawline and high cheekbones, but the hollow-eyed twist of his features sent a shiver down her spine. Dark blonde hair flowed back from his forehead. He had to be close to six feet tall. His t-shirt hung off of him like he'd lost a lot of weight, but the slenderness didn't seem to be affecting his strength any. His attention shifted to Pepper as she kept circling, putting the hood of car between them. That same low growl consumed the air again, stealing it away from her lungs. Pepper zoomed in on his face, making sure to get a good, identifiable shot, and blinked. The man had pale eyes, gray-green in color, and the pupils were clearly visible. Pepper's gaze jerked away from the screen to the man himself, to double-check what she'd seen through the lens, but he was too far away. She looked again, zooming in a little more. There. Vertical pupils, slit like a cat's even in the cloud-covered light.

"It is unwise to interfere in what you don't understand," he said quietly. It sounded like he was trying to be soothing. Pepper scoffed.

"Then tell me," she challenged. "No. Scratch that. I want *her* to tell me. Right now, on camera."

"He's trying to make me go with him. He says if I do, he won't hurt me, he'll make it good, and he's torn my clothes and please, please help me!" Pepper's heart turned over as the woman begged between sobs.

"The police are on their way," Pepper assured her. "They'll be here any second," she added and prayed that she was right. Pepper didn't want the situation to get any worse so she kept talking, stalling. "Hey, scumbag, you got a name? Or should I just keep making them up for you?"

That growl came again, louder this time, and Pepper realized it was actually coming from the attacker. Her heartbeat doubled in speed, but she smirked to cover it, keeping her phone up. The man turned toward her, pacing the length of the car with almost feline grace. Pepper shifted her grip to wipe the sweat from her palms. What was taking the police so long?

The attacker leaped over the hood, clearing it in a single smooth motion as Pepper jumped backward with a startled cry. She curled around her phone protectively, refusing to let the man near it. The growl closed around her. Hot breath curled across the back of her neck. He inhaled long and slow behind her ear, and chills slithered down her spine. A hand slid over her hair. He inhaled again, so close behind her that she could feel the heat of him through her polo shirt. Something scraped against the top of her head, back and forth, as a hand brushed over the curve of her hip. Pepper stomped, trying to drive her heel into the top of his foot, but she only met asphalt. Shock waves raced up her leg from impact and she wobbled. His hand tightened on her hip, dragging her backward and rumbling in her ear. There was pleasure in the sound. Pepper's stomach heaved.

As suddenly as he grabbed her, he was gone. Pepper didn't dare turn to look, instead straining her ears to listen. The sound of sirens filtered into the parking lot, quiet at first but growing steadily louder. The other woman sobbed and Pepper finally risked a glance around her. There was no sign of the attacker. Inch by inch, she lifted her head, searching warily around her with her phone still clutched to her chest. Her knuckles ached from the tension. He was gone. He was really gone. The strength went out of Pepper's knees, dropping her against the side of the car as she struggled to slow her heart. She stared with shocked, wide eyes as the black and white cruiser pulled into the parking lot.

A door slammed in the sudden stillness and Pepper spun. Abby strode from Turtle Rock like a gathering storm as the officers got out of their car. Pepper watched one glance from Abby's keen blue gaze take in the hysterical woman sobbing on the ground, as well as her own stunned expression. Abby shouldered the aluminum baseball bat in her hand and looked expectantly at Pepper. Her friend's voice held a distinct command. "Pepper?"

Pepper had the most absurd urge to giggle. She peeled her phone away from her chest.

"I got video," her voice was soft. A huge smile spread over her face as she danced in place. She slid into a triumphant shriek. "I actually got it on video!"

Abby stared at her. "Pepper, that was a seriously stupid thing to do," Abby said as she leaned on the bat like a cane. "You got halfway through a master's degree in criminology and you don't know better than to let the police handle things? You scared the hell out of me! Just what did you think you were going to do?"

"Get evidence," Pepper said smugly. "And I did." She held up her phone and waved it. She sighed, releasing as much of the pent-up adrenaline as she could. Her hands were starting to feel shaky. The recurring urge to giggle had to be the after-effects of adrenaline, and she coughed to clear the giddiness out of her throat. She leaned her head on Abby's shoulder for a moment. "Okay, so it wasn't the smartest thing to do, but I couldn't do *nothing*. All it takes for evil to succeed..."

"I know. I know. If I didn't know it before you started working here, I've certainly learned it since," Abby said with exasperated affection. She squeezed the younger woman around the shoulders. "Go home."

L. Dawn Jackson began writing stories as soon as they put a pencil in her chubby baby hand. She holds a bachelor's degree in English with a minor in creative writing, and was selected as a mentee in the 2021 Romance Authors Mentorship Program. She lives at the top of the American Rocky Mountains with two miracle children, her amazing husband, and an ever-increasing knitting stash. She can be found at theldawnjackson@gmail.com and on Facebook as L. Dawn Jackson.

Look for the rest of these stories and more as our contest winners and finalists grow their careers through the connections they make at the San Francisco Writers Conference.

Enter your work next time or join us at the next class or conference.

SFWriters.org

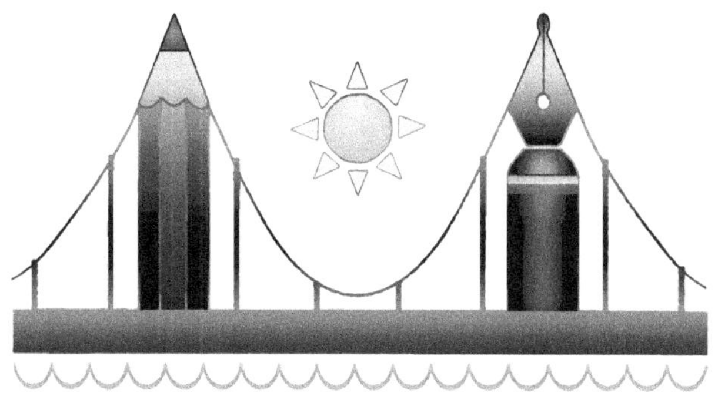

SAN FRANCISCO
WRITERS
CONFERENCE
Learn. Connect. Publish.

New Alexandria
CREATIVE GROUP